Praise for *Set Piece*

"*Set Piece* is a total delight—a layered tale of unexpected romance, family, and making room for what matters. I read it in a single sitting, right to the perfect Hollywood ending."

—Annabel Monaghan, best-selling author of *Same Time Next Summer* and *Nora Goes Off Script*

"Oh man, I gobbled up *Set Piece* in practically one sitting! Lana Schwartz's novella expertly crafts a dream scenario meet-cute—one that could be ripped straight from headlines. But *Set Piece* has more heart and more action than you'll ever get from *Us Weekly*."

—Lindsey Weber, cohost of *Who? Weekly*

"*Set Piece* is the whole, deeply enjoyable package, everything I'm always looking for in a romance: smart, warm, and sexy as all hell, full of characters to remember and root for. I loved it."

—Katie Cotugno, *New York Times* best-selling author

T0361622

Set
Piece

LANA SCHWARTZ

831 STORIES

831 Stories

An imprint of Authors Equity
1123 Broadway, Suite 1008
New York, New York 10010

Cover design by C47.
Book design by Scribe Inc.

This is a work of fiction. Names, characters, places and incidents either are products of the author's imagination or are used fictitiously.

Library of Congress Control Number: 2025930492
Print ISBN 9798893310351
Ebook ISBN 9798893310528

Printed in the United States of America
First printing

www.831stories.com
www.authorsequity.com

For Nora Nealis, the first person who taught
me to appreciate the magic of a good movie

1

Jack

On a small phone screen, I watch as a woman with almond-shaped eyes sticks her head out of the window of her posh Marylebone flat.

"Are you mad? Come out of the rain already," she calls out.

Then, the camera switches perspective.

A man stands in the street below. His white button-down shirt is drenched, revealing the outline of his chest and arms.

"I told you—I'm not going in there. You're coming out here," *he yells back, undeterred by the fat drops of rain falling from the sky.*

One of my hands goes to my face while the other moves to cover the phone screen, as if driven by instinct for self-preservation.

"Hey!" my mate George cries out next to me, shoving my palm off his phone. "I'm watching that!"

I feel my cheeks redden. Drawing my hand away is like fighting a losing battle with myself.

"It's *my* party, and I still haven't seen it." Tom reaches for the phone now, and George happily obliges.

"Alright, *alright*," I say, relenting and returning my hand to its rightful place—splayed across my eyes—so I won't have to see the action unfold in front of me. Suddenly, this dimly lit dive bar doesn't feel nearly dark enough.

The thing is, I don't need to see the phone to know what's about to happen between the woman and man on the screen because *I* am the man on the screen.

The woman, now giving into the man's demands, bursts out of her pastel-pink Victorian town house and flings herself into his arms. They kiss in the middle of the abandoned street, engulfed in each other and enraptured by the other's lips, teeth, and tongue. The man hoists the woman up by her hips and carries her, kissing still, across the threshold of her flat. He tosses her on the bed and stands over her.

He pulls her shirt over her head, then her skirt down her legs. Turning his attention to his own clothes, he feverishly unbuttons his shirt before tugging down his pants. Music soars in the background. He steps out of his trousers, then his boxers, revealing his giant, erect—

"OK," I say, snatching the phone out of Tom's grip. "That's enough."

Sitting there while my mates watch me act is bad enough, but being present for their reactions to the much-talked-about sex scene in the BBC show I costarred in and thought all of five people would see . . .

"Oh, come on. This is some of your finest work!" George laughs. "Jack Felgate's *biggest* role to date." He gives me a devilish grin.

I roll my eyes. "Yeah, well, tonight is about Tom."

Tom pushes his Clark Kent glasses up the bridge of his nose. "I'm perfectly fine with tonight being about you. Consider this your punishment for running off to settle the bill."

"Please. What kind of friend would I be if I let you pay the tab for your own stag party?"

"And you know he can afford it now," George quips. "Unlike the rest of us poor thespians."

I blush again. It's true, but I don't want to admit it.

"Next location?" I suggest, pulling Tom to his feet.

He stumbles slightly as he stands, and I take his tipsiness as a win. I worried when he insisted on a quiet celebration near his home in Pasadena with only a small group—the trio of us actors who'd met in London, plus his brother, Jim, and his future brother-in-law, Teddy—that he was keeping it low-key for my benefit. As grateful as I am that he's avoided the kind of weekend that could land me in the pages of the *Daily Mail* and give everyone another reason to talk, I want him to have a true night out.

"You good, mate?" I grip Tom's elbow as we head to the door.

"I am absolutely peachy." Tom taps my cheek. "I want you to know, Jack, that I am really, really proud of you."

"Thank you, Tom." He, George, and I met doing theater in uni, and over the last few years, they both felt that westward tug toward Los Angeles, leaving me by my lonesome in London. For a while, we were always up for the same roles, yet we somehow managed to keep a sense of humor if one of us nabbed it over the other.

"Don't tell George," he says in a stage whisper as we exit toward a hulking Uber, "but I always knew that you were going to be the famous one out of all of us. I read that script for *Flames Flickie Flick Flicker . . .*"

"*Flames Flicker Eternal.*"

"Yes. That one—and I knew that this one's special."

When I got the script for *Flames Flicker Eternal*—or *Flames*, as the fans now call it—I could sense there was something different about it. Production had already attached a British theater director known for her quiet, intimate plays with searing dialogue and an Oscar-nominated cinematographer with a flair for the romantic. But still, even the best BBC fare often flies under Americans' radar. I never expected that Netflix would pick it up. Or that its streaming debut would coincide with a February snowstorm in the Northeast that kept everyone at home for five days. Suddenly, what started as buzz about this clandestine love story reached a full-on frenzy that could not be ignored. My inbox was bursting with media opportunities and interview requests, and so was my costar Ginny's. Four months later, I'm getting offers without auditions, and for the first time in five years, my agent is paying me more good-news calls than she is sending "they went in another direction" emails.

As we make our way to our next location, our voices volley around the car, debating whether Man United can keep its edge over Liverpool. My phone buzzes from my jeans pocket, alerting me that I have too many emails to return and at least four missed calls from my team. It can wait. All of it.

"Ay, we're here," Teddy calls out from the front seat.

"What? Already?" I ask. We've been in the car for less than ten minutes. "Couldn't we have just walked?"

Everyone laughs. The driver most loudly.

"Welcome to Los Angeles," George says, swinging open the door.

My three previous trips had all been in service of bit parts, the kind of stuff I booked before *Flames Flicker Eternal* that barely justified the jet lag it brought on. I'd film all day and then retreat to whatever hotel I was being put up in near the set, my meals craft services or room service.

As I lead the charge and enter the redbrick building with the words Swan Dive hand-painted on the door, I take in the change of scenery: marble bar, art deco furnishings, and proper glassware in every hand. Despite the name, a dive this is not.

"Is that Jack Felgate?" a woman wearing a slip dress and holding a coupe whispers as we pass.

"*No way*," another whispers back. "He lives on a shire in England. Or something."

I look toward the bar, then back out at the group. *How can I get out of this?*

"Why don't we skip this one and move on to the next?" Tom throws me a life raft. As always.

"No, no, no." I shake my head. I can't let my hang-ups get in the way of Tom's good time.

Besides, I have a contingency plan. I knew I needed to prepare for the possibility I might be recognized. It's started to happen since the show came out. My favorite pub tipped off a paparazzo that I was a regular at Thursday night trivia, and pictures of me leaving were splattered across the internet. By the next week, trivia was mobbed with fans asking for selfies, and when I ran out of the bar panicked, onlookers told news outlets that I was rude and "too big for my britches." My first girlfriend shared with *The Sun* that she always knew I would make it. My year seven teacher gave an interview about what sort of student I was ("well-mannered" and "attentive"—in other words: unremarkable). Getting offers for roles with actors and directors I've dreamed of working with is thrilling. The rest of it is not.

I reach into my bag for a pair of fake glasses I'd grabbed at the pharmacy and a red beanie. It's June, but that hardly matters in Los Angeles.

"What the fuck is that?" George sizes me up in confusion. "Jesus Christ, man. Is that a *disguise*?"

Tom squints. "You look like Where's Wally."

"Worry about yourselves, yeah? Let's just go into the bar." I scan the crowd as we enter. Maybe those women were an aberration. Or everyone is just far too cool to care: This city is crawling with celebrities far bigger and more important than me. I clock an attractive bartender efficiently mixing drinks and fitting right in with the good-looking patrons.

My shoulders relax as we make our way to an empty table.

Until a woman steps in front of me, blocking my path. She's holding her iPhone, boasting a picture of a dog as white and fluffy as a cloud, inches from my face.

6

I hear her asking, fuzzy and as if through water, "You're Jack Felgate, aren't you? Will you take a picture with me?"

I force my vision to zoom out. The phone is connected to a hand, which is connected to an arm, which belongs to the voice asking me to confirm my identity. This is one of the women from before. Her eyes are wide. Frozen in place, I nod slowly.

"Bitch! I *told* you it was him!" she calls out to her friends, who rush over to join her. Their phones come at me as quickly as their questions do.

"Why are you wearing glasses? Do you wear glasses?"

"What are you doing *here*?"

"You *changed* my life in *Flames*. Did you know that?"

"Oh my God, you *cannot* be here. Do you come here all the time?"

"Will you *please* take a picture with us?"

I weigh my options and try to keep my expression placid. If I refuse to take photos, I will hurt their feelings, and I'll be branded a bad sport. But if I agree to, well, when does it stop?

I stand there, immobile, unable to make up my mind. My tongue is thick and heavy, my mouth dry.

"Hey! The private room you requested is ready and waiting for you." The bartender has left her post from behind the bar and is by my side. Her golden waves are stacked on top of her head, and she's wearing a simple black T-shirt and a pair of vintage-looking jeans that hang from her hips.

"Oh, sorry we're late. Ran into a bit of traffic," I say,

regaining sensation in my mouth and my limbs, like I'm coming down from an allergy attack.

"Well, come on." She nods to me before turning to the throng. "We're charging this man an exorbitant amount of money—I have to get him back there." She is both conspiratorial and firm.

As the first woman who approached me opens her mouth to object, the bartender continues, adjusting her hair. "And, of course, a round of drinks on the house for you ladies for being so accommodating."

The women exchange glances, and after about thirty seconds, it appears a consensus is reached. Their phones go back into purses, and I follow hot on my rescuer's trail.

"Is there really a back room?" I ask, hurrying closer to her.

"Please." She turns to look back at me. "I am a woman of my word."

She flashes me a bright smile, and my fingertips prickle in excitement.

"You're in luck," she says, punching in a door code. "Leo and Toby canceled last minute." She gestures for me to enter, and I know I'm supposed to take in the VIP grandeur of it, offer faint praise, at the very least. But I can't stop my eyes from landing on her.

The swath of her tan collarbone just visible at the neck of her shirt. The tiny diamond studs in her ears, somehow both sophisticated and no-nonsense. Her defined arms, strong . . . I want to know what from. Everything about her seems purposeful and controlled, except for her hair. She radiates gravitas—and also a warmth that suggests her skin would be hot to the touch. When she smiles again, her soft brown eyes crinkle with amusement, as if there is more she's holding back, and I want to know that too.

"Seriously? Leo and Toby?" I ask, remembering where I am.

"Well, no." She laughs. "But we did have a last-minute cancellation. It's all yours. I'll round up your friends."

"Let me give you my card."

"We can settle up at the end of the night." Her eyes search mine, and we both stand there a beat longer than is natural. Like she might be keen on me too.

"What's your name?" she asks.

So she doesn't recognize me.

"Jack Felgate. And you?"

"Cara."

I hold out my hand, and she put hers in mine. I shake it slowly. I was right. Her skin sets mine on fire.

II

Cara

"Why are you looking at me like that?" I ask Katia, the other bartender working tonight, as I cut a fresh batch of limes. She has a smirk on her face that suggests she caught me red-handed for a minor crime I have no idea I committed.

She shakes her head and smiles. "Cara, I saw the way you darted over there to meet Jack Felgate." She rinses a cocktail shaker. "And I can't say I blame you. I probably would've done the same if I'd been a little quicker to the punch."

"What are you talking about?" Now that we're out of the 9 p.m. rush, we can have a conversation that isn't strictly about passing each other bottles or getting out of each other's way.

I grab more citrus, even though we probably have enough to get us through the night. I need something to do with my hands. Physically, I'm behind the bar, but my brain is still back in the room I'd just left.

"The man you just saved from those women." She takes a sip of her soda and bitters.

I respond with a blank expression.

"You really are hopeless, aren't you?" She laughs. "Just being aware that there *are* TV shows is all I'm asking."

Katia and I are behind the bar together three times a week. She's an aspiring music supervisor—a goth with pale skin, dark hair, and signature kohl eyeliner—who doesn't care what medium she's watching as long as it has a good soundtrack. Until recently, I was an aspiring production designer. You'd be hard-pressed to find a bartender in Los Angeles who isn't an aspiring something.

This is a bit of ours: She streams every new show the week it debuts, and I glean most of my inspiration from films that predate the new millennium. These days, I'm more cartoonishly out of the loop than usual, surviving solely on old comfort watches: screwball comedies, MGM musicals, and the kind of '90s character-driven mid-budget films they don't make anymore.

"OK, but seriously, Cara, everyone is obsessed with this BBC show, *Flames Flicker Eternal.* And that hot guy you escorted to our back room happens to be the star," Katia says, giving me side-eye. "You really didn't recognize him?"

From across the bar, all I could see was a good-looking guy who I assumed must have some modicum of clout, given that he was about to be mauled if someone didn't intervene. But when I stood next to him, I understood why these women were overcome, even in a city where famous people live, party, and shop at Gelson's among us.

Jack is handsome, but in a way that suggests he's equally likely to show up throwing rocks at a window as to play the male lead in a British drama. He's taller than average, but not so tall I had to crane my neck to look at him; he has a lean and muscular build, but not one that suggests he subscribes to some sort of all-consuming fitness and diet routine; he has a square jaw and an 11 p.m. shadow, with wide-set cheekbones, wavy brown hair, and light-green eyes. If Jack were in a boy band, he would be the second-best but still-good-looking member who somehow feels attainable, against all odds. I smile to myself, thinking about the "not-like-other-girls" superiority complex I carried around in middle school because Ramsey was my favorite member of Mischief instead of Charlie.

"Give me your phone," Katia demands, and I comply. "Take your fifteen minutes. Don't come back until you've watched this at least twice."

"Are those doctor's orders?" There is a video queued up: "The STEAMIEST Sex Scene in Flames Flicker Eternal!!!"

"And you might want to watch it in the staff bathroom, where you can have"—Katia notices a customer angling for her attention—"privacy." She punctuates the end of her sentence with a wink.

Ignoring her, I head out the side door into the alleyway. I lean against the building's facade, feeling the roughness of the brick through my shirt.

No new texts or missed calls since my last glance at my phone an hour ago. I exhale fully, not realizing I had been holding my breath until I do. No news is good news.

I hit play and prepare for what I always experience when I watch a new-to-me movie or show: my tendency to dissect it. Having spent years on sets, all I see is the devil in the details: I can picture what the shot list looked like, the conversations about locations, the crew just off-camera.

On the screen in front of me, an actress goes outside and meets Jack's character in the rain. He hoists her up and carries her across the threshold. But instead of thinking about the camera transitions from an exterior on a London street to the interior of a carefully built set, my brain snags on the ferocity in Jack's eyes. There's a rawness I've found lacking among other contemporary actors.

I wonder how those hands would feel on my hips, I think, blushing, then, *What an embarrassing thought*, blushing even more.

Jack carries the actress to her bed, pulls off her clothes, and strips his. I suck in my breath as he reveals his defined chest, a smattering of dark hair across it. As he begins to lower his boxer briefs, I feel my heartbeat quicken. I still, as if I'm afraid to startle the people on the screen. I wait to see just how far down they'll go.

Oh shit. He's about to go full frontal. I refuse to blink.

Then, the video cuts out.

What the fuck. I tap anxiously at the screen, trying to convince it to continue through the sheer force of my will. But it hasn't stalled; it's ended. I reposition myself, pressing more of my back against the brick wall behind me. I hit play on the video and watch it again. And again.

At the end of my break, I stride back inside and reassume my position next to Katia, the expression on my face as inscrutable as the movie *Inception*. I'm good at concealing my feelings, but I'm usually masking anger or frustration, not desire.

"So, what did you think?" she asks almost tauntingly as she scoops ice into a shaker.

I scan the bar for the group of women who had swarmed Jack earlier, still riding the high of their brief encounter. I look toward the unmarked door to the private room, where I left Jack and his friends. He's handsome, and he can act, but so what? Good for him.

"Their use of shadows in the bedroom was really interesting—I wonder who the gaffer is," I say, yanking a vague observation from some dim corner of my mind.

Katia rolls her eyes and tilts her head toward a customer. "You, my friend, are impossible."

Another person approaches the bar, then another, and another. And I am grateful to them for distracting Katia but also me.

Only at 1:45 a.m., last call, does the bar start to empty out. When it's Katia and me working, we take turns closing solo, and tonight I'm saddled with one lingering couple, their legs intertwined at a high top.

As I wipe down a red wine spill, I hear footsteps approaching.

"Just so you know, we're closing in fifteen minutes," I call out, back turned, wanting to cut them off at the pass.

"That's fine," I hear a mild British voice say above me. "I was hoping to settle up, if that's alright."

I look at Jack standing over me. All night, I've carried an awareness of his presence in the back room. Yet having him in front of me feels like a total surprise, like I've conjured him here out of thin air. I reflexively drop the rag in my hand. The warmth I felt on my cheeks earlier returns with a vengeance, there to remind me that I, like 1.2 million others, have watched—and enjoyed—Jack's STEAMIEST Sex Scene in Flames Flicker Eternal!!! Or at least its prelude.

I track his glances around the bar as he gauges if it really is as empty as it seems.

"Don't worry," I say, gesturing toward the remaining couple, hands all over each other as they stumble to their feet. "I don't know if they've seen your show, but I think they were about to give us one."

Jack laughs, revealing a set of perfectly straight teeth, each one working to debunk any stereotypes about British dental care.

"Oh right, your check, with a discount," I say, shaking my head, feeling my hair loosening, like it's aching to come down.

"No, no discount," he says, the corner of his mouth quirking. "You were a lifesaver; you have no idea."

"And you have no idea how happy the owners will be when they hear I saved an actor from getting Mufasa'd at their fine establishment."

"I do consider myself more of a Timon," he jokes, passing me his card. His wrist brushes against my thumb, and though we shook hands earlier, I feel this touch in my entire body. He sticks his card back in his wallet and his wallet in his back pocket. I follow these actions like there's something novel about them.

We stand there silently, facing each other. Our eyes meet. The bar is almost completely silent now. No music, no lively conversation. It's the particularly pronounced quiet of a place typically filled with sound.

My brain splits into two warring factions: The smarter, sharper side wants to come up with an excuse to prolong Jack's visit, and the other is busy counting his eyelashes.

He opens his mouth to speak, and I can tell he's on the verge of asking me *something* consequential. I can see it in his eyes. I can feel it on the tip of his tongue. I can—

"Hey, are you ready to go or what?" Jack's friend asks as the group of them spills out of the back room to retrieve him.

Whatever words Jack was about to speak are lost.

I'd been so distracted by Jack's presence that I forgot he had a whole crew to contend with.

The drunkest of them, the bachelor of the evening, puts his hand on Jack's shoulder. "*You* are seriously the best," he says. "And thank *you*." He points at me.

The group starts out the door. My eyes flicker to Jack, who looks between his friends and me like he's watching a tennis match. He follows them out the door.

I sigh, feeling a bubble of disappointment balloon in

my chest and then annoyance for setting myself up for this disappointment. *I don't have time for distractions right now anyway*, I tell myself as I drag two giant trash bags to the dumpster.

I have more important things going on, I chide as I run through my mental checklist—lights out, music off, safe secured—and grab my bag.

I barely have time to work at this bar, let alone seduce actors who patronize it, I remind myself as I unlock the front door to leave and lock it behind me again.

My eyes land on a shadow looming under the awning.

Instinctively, I reach for the pepper spray in my purse, primed to make a run for it to my car if needed.

I see square shoulders, chestnut hair. Jack's square shoulders, Jack's chestnut hair. I bite back a smile.

"I'm aware of the irony of asking a bartender this," he starts, "but might I be able to buy you a drink?"

III

Cara

I knew I hadn't wanted Jack to leave when he did, but it hadn't occurred to me what might happen if he'd stayed.

"I have just the place for a drink. Heard of Swan Dive?" I ask, jerking my thumb behind me without breaking eye contact. "On the house, even." I hold the door open for him. The corner of his mouth turns up again, and my body starts humming at a low frequency.

I check the clock on the wall. 2:15 a.m.

My broken-in Blundstones lead me back behind the bar. I can't remember the last time my body moved faster than my brain.

By fifteen minutes after close, I should be pulling down the grate out front; by 2:45 a.m., I should be at my front door; by 3 a.m., I should be allowing my exhaustion from an eight-hour shift to carry me off to sleep. By 10 a.m., I have to be at my mom's apartment to make sure she's eaten and taken her meds. I feel a pang in my stomach. How will I be able to do all of that if I don't go home right now?

One hour, I tell myself. I can have a drink with this man for one hour. Years of long days on sets prepared me to do a lot on a little sleep.

"Should I lock this?" Jack asks, gesturing toward the entrance.

I nod. He turns the dead bolt, a consideration I find oddly touching and sexy, and slides onto a stool. Now that we're the only two people here, I can't covertly watch him from a distance, and I don't know where to look.

"What can I get you?" I ask, falling back into my role of cocktail slinger to calm my nerves.

"Oh, whatever you have will do." Jack rests his elbows on the marble surface and traces a hairline crack with his thumb. My brain, clearly stuck on the video it watched hours ago, registers it as a strikingly sensual gesture.

"It's a bar. We have *everything*." I try for easy, amused, but I have to look away from him to hide my blush.

"What are you in the mood for?"

"No, no, no. This decision is yours and yours alone."

"Then . . . tequila. On the rocks." He nods decisively. His eyes are on my neck and my arms.

"Tequila is good," I agree simply. *What is it about being in front of him that whittles my vocabulary down to fifteen words? Like if I say more, I'll completely unravel.* I'm not used to feeling off-kilter in the presence of an actor, and his star power isn't what's destabilizing me. I've been around plenty of "talent"—and enough to know that he has *it*, but he also doesn't wield that like a weapon.

"Oh yeah, I can't get enough of the stuff," Jack says, then

pauses. He clears his throat. "Not in, like, a problematic way. It's just . . . that's my go-to drink."

I laugh. Is he nervous? My brain tingles pleasantly at the prospect.

My eyes skim our tequila labels. Clase Azul. I place it on the counter with relish, and I pour us both a few fingers over ice. Two hours ago, my exhaustion felt like a thumb pressing down on me, and now I have enough energy to power the engine of a small car.

"Cheers." He clinks his glass against my own.

"Cheers? Isn't that how Brits say goodbye?"

"Hello, goodbye, thanks, you name it," he says with a laugh. "Not to be confused with cheerio, which *only* means goodbye." He spins his glass. "Constantly having to educate Americans."

"That's why we declared independence. So we wouldn't have to know any of this."

"I thought it was so you didn't have to pay taxes."

"Common misconception." I take a sip. The cold, salty liquor hardly matters at this point. My head is already at high altitude. I hadn't bothered to turn the lamps back on, and our faces are illuminated by the light filtering in from the street.

"God, that's smooth," Jack remarks in surprise. "So, are you going to have a drink with me or one over there?" His chin gestures to the far side of the bar separating us.

The barstool next to him is innocuous. Wooden back, leather seat. But accepting his invitation to sit there, next to him, feels like unlocking the next level in a video game.

Like I've found a cheat code that will allow me to inhabit the carefree lifestyle of a twenty-nine-year-old woman who *isn't* shuttling her sick mother back and forth between chemo treatments at Cedars-Sinai.

Without replying, I walk out from behind the bar and slip into the seat, resting my feet on the bar between the stool's legs. We're facing each other now, his knees bracketing mine.

"You've never had this before?" I ask, turning my attention to our drinks to keep it off anything else. Clase Azul is a bottle service tequila of choice.

"No, I'm afraid my tastes aren't much finer than Montezuma."

"You're telling me you don't drink anything nicer than Montezuma?" I find this hard to believe—a performative celebrity move, maybe, like when models eat cheeseburgers during magazine interviews. "Really?"

"No, why would I?" His thumb traces circles around the rim of the glass. I watch it move with interest.

"Common decency for one."

"Ouch!" he counters in mock offense.

"I'm very sorry," I say in a tone that suggests I am not very sorry at all. "That was below the belt. Do you Brits have that phrase?"

"We do." Jack leans forward. "But it means something completely different." The warmth spreads from my cheeks to my chest, and I am grateful for the bar's relative darkness.

"Well, certainly you can afford better tequila now that you're *the next big thing*," I say in what I hope is a breezy, casual voice. But Jack just looks down at his glass, now cradled in his hands.

Shit. "I didn't mean—" I sound . . . starry-eyed. Like the women who were gushing over him. "Drink whatever you like. Expensive doesn't mean better."

"No, no, it's not that." He pauses for a beat, gazes back up at me, and narrows his eyes as if to really take me in. "How do I explain this? It's like my life is happening without any sort of input from me. The wheels are moving, and I'm strapped to the top of the car."

I understand this so well it feels uncanny. But that's more than I'm prepared to let on. Instead, I take a too-big gulp of my drink and cough, pushing down thoughts of anything that doesn't involve the two of us here, now.

"I mean, not that I'm not grateful for these opportunities. I am . . . it's just . . ."

"It's like you're watching your life happen to you instead of living it," I say, measured.

"Exactly." Jack peers at me slightly differently now, as though I'd peeled back a layer of my skin.

We sit in silence for a moment, waiting to see what the other might do or say to fill it.

"The way you got those women off my case, though, that was brilliant. Have you considered working in security? Bouncer instead of bartender?"

"You'd be surprised what you're capable of when you use a firm, authoritative voice."

Jack nods, taking this information in like it had never occurred to him before.

"And that's something you picked up working here?"

I shake my head. "On set, actually." He cocks an eyebrow. I get ahead of his next question. "I'm not an actor. I'm in set design. But I started as a PA, then worked in different art department roles until I could work my way up to production designer. Bartending is something I do . . . between gigs . . ." I don't want to reveal the specific circumstances that necessitated my side hustle to usurp my main one. *What was the definition of insanity? Telling a hot guy you just met about your mom's cancer diagnosis.*

Now, both of Jack's eyebrows are raised in appraisal. He waits for me to continue.

"I noticed, working on all of these sets, which department heads and directors are best at getting people to respect them. It's not the people who jump up and down and scream or throw these wild tantrums and act like divas. It's the people who ask for what they want clearly and confidently."

Jack looks straight into my eyes while he mulls this over. "You're absolutely right. And the yellers and screamers—if I'm ever like that, you can go ahead and off me. Right then and there."

"Jack, you seem really nice . . . but I don't think I'm ready for that kind of commitment," I say, proud of myself for volleying back. It's nice to banter—it makes me feel more like myself than I have in a while.

"And they always say it's men who can't commit." Jack flashes that same wide smile from earlier, and I bask in it.

"Well, correct me if I'm wrong, but don't you have a big hit on your hands . . . from what I can tell?"

"So, does this mean you've seen my show?" He's practically wincing.

I choose my next words with surgical precision, thinking back to watching the prelude to his sex scene, my back up against the wall.

"I've seen . . . parts of it."

"It's just . . . I grew up watching these forces of nature . . . like Denzel Washington and Daniel Day-Lewis. Actors who have these storied careers. Now every week there's another article about how movies are dead, and there are more 'next big things' than there are actual things—successes. It's hard to know if you're building something real or if this is—if *I* am—a flash in the pan."

I nod. "When I was a kid, my mom would show me all of these old MGM musicals like *On the Town* and *An American in Paris*, with all of these big, beautiful sets. As soon as I learned that someone was in charge of creating them, I knew that's what I was going to do. But now that I'm actually getting to do it, I realize sets like those—they're of another time."

"I love those movies too!" Jack says excitedly, his knee knocking into mine. "I took a film history course at uni about the studio system in the States, and they were required viewing. I got hooked."

"They're the best." I suppress my urge to ask his opinion of every movie he's ever seen. "And now studio execs blame audiences for not flocking to movies where everything looks flat or fake . . ." I trail off when I realize how intently Jack is watching me. Our glasses of tequila are drained, and we've inched our bodies closer, angling toward each other. There are no nervous ticks, no furtive eye movements. I allow myself to sit and steep in this stillness. To soak up the warmth of his attention. To feel my body's response to it. I'm buzzing, and I know it's not the tequila.

"Well, I'd love to see some of your work sometime, Cara." He pronounces it *Cahr-a*, like "car," instead of how it's meant to be said, like "care." Someone saying my name wrong never sounded so good.

"Cara," I respond, correcting.

"*Cah-ra.*"

"Cara."

"*Cah-ra.*"

"You might want to hold off on accepting any parts where you play an American. Your accent still needs work."

"What?!" he scoffs, incredulous. "What kind of dialect coach are you? This is not very encouraging."

"You're right. I'm sorry." I squeeze his forearm where the edge of his rolled-up shirt cuff meets his skin and feel his lean muscle against my fingers. He catches my eye with a smirk. I drop my hand abruptly, as if I've been caught. "I should be more encouraging. Be the Rex Harrison to your Eliza Doolittle."

"So I'm the fair lady?" He shifts forward in his seat, the insides of his thighs grazing my knees as he does.

I slide forward too, and my legs press between his.

"Well, *obviously*. But that's only my third-favorite Cukor." I move away my empty glass, and a section of my hair falls loose.

"May I?" Jack asks, his hand pausing halfway to my face. I nod. He tucks the wave behind my ear. Then he drags a finger down my neck and traces the outline of my clavicle. I bask in his touch. My entire body perks up.

"So. What's your favorite Cukor?" he whispers. It's quite possibly the hottest question he could have asked me. I answer by pressing my mouth to his. His tongue finds mine, and he stands, pulling my face into his, his hands cradling my head. His mouth is on my earlobe, then my neck, and back to my lips. I can't think about anything but where it will land next.

Jack pulls away, his thumb smoothing over my cheek, and I feel dizzy, like the room has been pressurized.

"Is this OK?" he asks, reaching under the hem of my T-shirt and searching my eyes.

"Yes." I lean into him. My hands rake down his back. He drops his head and kisses my breasts through my shirt before pulling it over my head, revealing a simple black bra.

"My God, you're really beautiful," he murmurs as he takes me in, and I want to do the same to him.

"Your turn," I tell him, and he lifts his shirt over his head and tosses it on the floor. I've seen his chest like this before, three times exactly. But never at scale.

I kiss him harder this time. I lean my chest into his as he palms my lower back, and the pressure of our bodies meeting sends a current through me.

Before I can adjust to the thrill, he hoists me onto the empty bar.

"I've always wanted to do that," he says, visibly impressed

by his own execution, as he reaches for the button of my 501s and pulls down the zipper. I plant my hands on the bar behind me and lift my ass off the marble surface so he can slide the jeans down, and he slings them over a barstool.

He traces the edges of my underwear, first with his finger, then with his tongue. He moans like he's the one being touched. The ache between my legs is so strong it's almost painful.

I reach for his waistband.

"Jack, I want you to fuck me," I tell him before I consciously have the thought.

"Oh, I'm going to. But you'll have to be patient. Can you do that?" I nod in response. I feel myself flush.

He unhooks my bra, then kisses my neck, my shoulder, the crease of my elbow, my naked breasts, my navel. He kisses me through my soaked underwear, and when I reach for his belt buckle, he gives me a stern look, moves just out of my reach, and slips a finger into me. I gasp at the suddenness of it, and he grins, satisfied, eyes glowing. Like he senses he knows what I need more than I do. He might. He props my feet on the backs of our barstools and pulls my hips forward. When he pushes my underwear to the side and bends to lick me, he moans again, and it reverberates through every cell in my body. If I think about the fact that I'm getting head from a TV actor on a bar, it feels absurd, so I force myself to stay in the moment and merely *enjoy* the fact that I'm getting head from a TV actor on a bar. His tongue glides over my clit, and any prospect of thinking at all dissipates.

He grips the back of my knee to hold me still, and I let my head dip over the back side of the bar. Something falls—cocktail stirrers, napkins—I'm too caught up to discern the sound. I'm sprawled and open, and my awareness of that brings me closer.

"Oh, look, she can let go." His teeth graze my inner thigh, and he uses two fingers to bring me over the edge. Ripples of pleasure break into waves crashing over the length of my body. My eyes blur, and all I can see is the sheen of sweat across his chest.

"*Jack, fuck me,*" I beg.

I hear the clink of metal, his belt buckle hitting the floor. When I look up, he's naked except for gray cotton briefs, a wet spot in front where his dick was aching for escape while he was going down on me. He climbs onto the bar, slightly clumsily—adorably clumsily—and I catch the glint of a condom wrapper in his hand.

I reach for him, and this time he lets me. My breath hitches in my rib cage; I am about to get the big reveal, and I slide my hands into his waistband so I can feel it before I see it.

"No wonder those women were excited to see you."

"What do you mean? I thought they liked me for my personality."

I smirk, and he does too. I like both the feel of his dick in my hand and being able to tease him while I'm holding him.

"OK, you've had a laugh. Now I am going to fuck you, Cara."

Cah-ra. And I'm back to following his lead, something I so rarely do.

He frees himself from his underwear, slips on the condom, and, with his hands on my hips, starts to coax himself gently inside me. His face hangs inches above mine, and he takes a few slow, deep breaths, the warmth of them hitting my cheeks, before he thrusts into me fully. In search of a way to steady myself, one of my hands finds the edge of the bar, and the other finds his ass.

"Fuck," Jack cries out, muffling his own response by kissing me, his mouth more feverish now. The excitement of this night and this theatrically hot sex has us both at the brink. I hold him tighter and pull him deeper, wanting to make it the *most*. To sate myself fully. For a long time.

I feel Jack erupt inside me, and I wrap my legs around his waist. I tilt my head back and close my eyes, and he kisses my chin with a tenderness that doesn't suit our situation: the two of us, only slightly more than strangers, lying spent on the surface where I poured glasses of Pinot an hour ago.

I wrap my arms around his back, squeezing him closer and keeping him inside of me, as if that can stop time. As if lingering inside this bubble we've created might prevent me from having to contend with all of the complications that exist outside of it. I'm not used to sex feeling transportive in this way, and I don't want it to end.

"Would you come back to my hotel with me?" he asks, his breath still short, only now making its way back into his chest. I can feel the blood returning to my limbs as I contemplate where they'll take me next.

I know I shouldn't, that I ought to go home to my own bed. But I said yes to so many things tonight that I wouldn't normally consider—a drink with Jack, a kiss with Jack, sex with Jack—what's one more yes?

I nod. "But I have to do one thing first."

"What's that?"

"Bleach this bar."

IV

Jack

"Kurtz put it together over at Sony."

"Kurtz and who? Have they confirmed a distribution plan yet?"

"It's Kurtz and Ryman from that indie company Broken Glass Pictures. Nothing confirmed yet, but they're looking at a limited run in theaters, then streaming."

I groan.

"What's that sound?" the voice on the other end of the phone asks.

"That's just Jack. Sorry, Carmen, you're on speaker with both of us."

My agent, Delia Browning, sits next to me in the back of a black car, straight off a twelve-hour flight from Heathrow to LAX. I am exhausted, but Delia is a general ready to go to war. I reach for the eye drops in my jacket pocket.

"Who did the script?" Delia presses.

"The Patels—husband and wife couple, big in TV, making

31

the jump to features. The studio asked for their take on *The Great Gatsby*."

"They're remaking that *again*?" I whisper to Delia in disbelief.

She hushes me and continues on, unabated. "Who's directing?"

"It's Gray," Carmen replies, keyboard clacking in the background.

"Wait, Gray has this?" Delia sits up even taller. Gray was a huge director in the '80s, responsible for some of the decade's biggest blockbusters and action flicks. Now, he only works sporadically, returning for a pet project or simply when he feels like it.

"If it's Gray, it's a no-brainer," Delia says, more to me than to Carmen.

"Well, not *that* Gray. Gray's son, Timmy. The festival-circuit darling. Longest standing ovation in Cannes history."

Delia raises her brows at me, and I know how I'm meant to read this face. But I meet Delia's excitement with reluctance. I have another movie starting production in a few months. If I take this on now, I will have almost no downtime between projects.

Carmen continues, typing away. "Listen, if Jack doesn't want it, it's OK. But we need to find our new Nick fast." Then, she evokes her Hail Mary: "Alden Ehrenreich's people are already circling."

Delia arches her left eyebrow even higher. She presses mute.

"Well-known TV couple, director who isn't afraid to take risks. A fresh take on popular IP. And Broken Glass has been selling movies for record prices at Sundance and TIFF. Given the timing, I suspect they'll do a full-court press for this. I don't really see a downside here, Jack."

I chew my lip and assess Delia. Her jet-black hair is pulled into a perfect bun that somehow survived a transcontinental flight. I don't even think she slept on the plane.

We first met nine years ago when she saw me in a production of *Mother Courage and Her Children*. Not one agent had ever offered me representation before, despite plenty of effort on my part. Delia was the one who got me the audition for *Flames Flicker Eternal* when casting wasn't interested in seeing me. She hasn't steered me wrong since.

She continues applying pressure with ease: "Do you really want Alden Ehrenreich stealing all your buzz?"

I roll my eyes and shake my head, grinning despite myself.

Delia doesn't smile with her mouth, but I can see the delight of a deal in her eyes.

She unmutes the phone.

"Email me the script immediately," she demands.

"One more thing," I chime in. "Can we find out who's on hair and makeup, costumes, and production design?" If a *Gatsby* remake looks cheap, I know how it will fare. I might not have the leverage to *do* anything about it, but I still want to know.

"Rachel Miles is on hair. Karen Sun for makeup."

Delia nods. "All solid," she whispers to me assuredly.

"And for production design CJ Ericson, just off *The Bee's Knees*."

"*Oh yes!*" Delia exclaims with recognition. "Haven't seen it yet, but it was at South By and picked up a ton of word of mouth," she adds for my benefit.

I nod at her, and she knows what to say.

"Send the contract over."

She and Carmen continue their conversation, but my thoughts drift to the Sunset Tower Hotel, where my team has arranged for me to stay. All I can think about is closing the thick, cream curtains and crawling into the giant bed, waking up only to order room service until I come out on the other side of my jet lag.

All of my trips to LA have been short, oversaturated bursts. A few days here, a week there, never really enough time to see the city in any real way. The closest I've come to anything of substance was Tom's bachelor party five years ago. My mind catches on the events of that weekend. The bar, the bartender. Even now, my eyes scan the credits of new releases to see if I might catch a "Cara" in the art department. A few years back, I looked up Swan Dive and was half relieved to see it had closed, preventing me from doing anything daft like showing up to ask after her.

I roll down the car's tinted window, expecting to be met with darkness. We've been traveling for so long that the fact that it's morning here comes as a surprise. I wince at the sun and the stream of cars inching along the freeway, but I soften at the palm trees that loom over it.

Now off the phone with Carmen, Delia turns to me. "How early can I set a meeting tomorrow? How wild are you planning on getting at the People's Choice after-parties?"

I snort. My phone dings. Amid the sea of notifications, I spot a text that reads "See you tonight xx."

"Ginny will be there?" I ask Delia.

She looks at me surprised, almost offended.

"I made sure of it."

V

CJ

The coffee shop patio is buzzing with toned and tanned people chatting animatedly, sipping iced Americanos and matcha lattes, taking pregnant pauses before unloading a particularly chewy piece of gossip. The trees around the patio's perimeter give a false sense of privacy but real shade, a prize on this scorchingly hot Los Angeles day.

It's exactly the kind of place Stuart hates, so why he asked me to drive all the way out here to West Hollywood is beyond me.

When I arrive, squinting through my sunglasses, I find him reading a copy of *Artforum*. His salt-and-pepper hair is slicked back, and the top three buttons of his light-pink linen shirt, which have never been put to use, continue to lie at ease. He is thirty years older than everyone here, but Stuart would stand out anywhere.

"For me?" I ask, reaching for one of the coffees on the table and sliding into the bistro chair across from him. The warmth of the seat announces itself against the ridges of my micro-pleat pants.

"Well, despite all of my overtures, Hugh Grant still refuses to meet me, so yes." Stuart's British accent has diminished after fifty years in the States but not vanished.

"I'm lucky Hugh and I have the same coffee order."

Stuart closes the magazine and places it on the table with flourish, the very same manner in which he does most things. "Nice to see you outside of your zip code."

"I leave Eagle Rock! I went to that black box theater," I say defensively.

"That was in Highland Park. Two months ago. With *me*."

"Well, once production on *Gatsby* starts next week, I'll be away constantly. Which I don't feel great about."

"By the way, I would've been happy to put a call in about that gig, and you know it. Kurtz is an old friend."

I shake my head. We've been over this. So many times. "I have an agent. I don't want your help with jobs."

"Oh, yes, no one gets any favors in this town. It runs on pure talent and hard work," Stuart says, dripping with sarcasm. "Plus, Kurtz really does owe me. I practically saved his life at Danceteria."

"You really were the Forrest Gump of the '80s, weren't you?"

Stuart holds up his hand to stop me. "Please do not bring that movie up in front of me. You know how I feel about it."

"You didn't tell Kurtz though, right?"

"Tell Kurtz what?"

"That I'm your daughter?"

"I thought that would be up to you to tell him, if you want." Stuart's tone softens, and I feel the muscles in my neck and shoulders release. I always get tense—nervy—when we go down this road.

"Can I show you the sets?"

He leans in, and I open my phone, pulling up an album and scrolling. "This is Daisy's drawing room: lots of glass. You know, beautiful but transparent."

"Oh, that lace—the color. It's good."

"We dyed it."

"Exquisite," he says, a proud look on his face. "Makes me wish I was still directing movies so that *I* could hire you."

"Like I'd ever let you." I say this with the cadence of a joke, but it's true. "Besides, if this goes well, you wouldn't be able to afford me."

"That's exactly what I'm hoping for."

"I just have to stay focused. Make the most of this," I say, more for my own benefit than Stuart's.

"Darling, no one would ever argue that you lack focus. Listen, Agnes is a good age for you to be doing this." He leans in and looks at me sincerely, redirecting the conversation to where he knows my real fears lie. "Four is when you start to have memories that carry into adulthood. Now she's going to get to see what else her mother is capable of."

My phone, face down, buzzes. I look at the notifications decorating my lock screen, obscuring a recent photo of Agnes in unicorn face paint. I can't believe it's been four years since she was born. Five years since I lost my mom.

"Felgate Gets Green Light, Picks Up Pattinson's Role in Gray *Gatsby*," the *Variety* headline reads. Underneath is Jack's headshot photoshopped next to one of Robert

Pattinson, who was set to be our Nick Carraway, the moral center of the story. Plenty of actors would tell you that Nick, the audience surrogate, is actually the better part than the titular role; Jack Felgate is apparently one of them.

My cheeks flush, and I put down my coffee.

Stuart peers at me curiously.

"There's been a casting shake-up. The part of Nick Carraway will now be played by . . . Jack Felgate."

Stuart raises his eyebrows so high they are practically in his hairline. "That's the Jack you had the one-night stand with?"

I put my palm on my forehead. "Why did I tell you that?"

"Because sometimes, like your father, you drink too many margaritas."

"I could've sworn I got that from my mom."

"No, you get all of your good traits from her, and all the questionable ones come from me."

In the years since we met, it feels like Jack has become omnipresent. The trades are constantly tracking his career moves, there are in-depth profiles about his rise as a Hollywood It Boy, and despite a minimal online presence, he is constantly going viral for the cardigan he's wearing, the flowers he's buying at a market in London, the book that's peeking out of his back pocket. I haven't been able to bring myself to watch anything else he's been in—or even the entirety of *Flames*. Reckoning with the reality of my feelings about him—the way the memory of that night has refused to recede in my consciousness, the physical reaction I have to seeing photos of him—feels both terrifying and juvenile.

When I look at photos of him, I see the man with whom I briefly cast aside my responsibilities for a fling that felt improbably joyful and exhilarating at the time and even more so now. Everything about those last few months of my mother's life is a blur, except for that night. To me, Jack represents a one-night-only taste of youthful exuberance before all of my experiences were cast in the shadow of grief. Ours was a connection at a time when I desperately needed one: a reprieve from the devastation I felt and the future loss I couldn't even conceive of. Sometimes I wonder if there might have been something real between us, but then I remind myself that the intensity of my life during that period colored everything I experienced. Like the volume was turned up on every encounter, every interaction.

My cheeks warm, and not from the sun. There's so much Jack brings up for me, and I don't need to go there.

"Well, I'm glad you remember this story, but there's no way Jack does," I assure Stuart.

"You are exceedingly memorable," Stuart says. "That you get from both your mother and me."

"Momma, I need you."

I open Agnes's bedroom door, toothbrush in my mouth, to find her exactly as I left her minutes earlier.

I sit at the edge of her bed and smooth her hair. An unruly

blond mop, a few shades lighter than mine, along with giant, unblinking brown eyes. Mine too.

"What is it, sweetie?"

"I woke up, and I didn't know where you were."

"You mean to tell me that in the last *three* minutes, you already fell asleep and woke back up?"

"I don't know!"

"That means there's still *plenty* of time for us to get lots and lots of sleep and be ready for school tomorrow." I wrap one of her curls around my ring finger.

"And Uncle Stuart is going to take me *and* pick me up."

"That's right." It isn't a secret that Stuart is her grand-father, but something about the term "Grandpa" doesn't feel quite right. "But I'll be home for dinner. With the good pizza." I realize I am making these assurances as much for myself as for her.

I kiss her on the temple and tuck her into the sheets that the costumer on my last job embroidered with her name—a special wrap gift for me. I gently close her door to force myself to bed as well.

I'm plagued by the "night before the first day of school" jitters that starting a movie always gives me. Much of the work has already been done in preproduction; the sets designed and mostly constructed, props selected. But still my heart ping-pongs knowing how impossible it is to gauge how any of it will look until the director begins shooting. Other films I've been on, I didn't need to show up every day, but this one is different. This is my biggest budget, my biggest departments, my biggest swing. Also the most time I'll have spent away from Agnes for work. If all goes well, this movie will be my calling card, and if it doesn't, the guilt I'm already wracked with will be double.

Tossing and turning, I look over at the clock: 11 p.m.

I reach for my phone on my nightstand and do something I don't ever allow myself to do: google Jack.

There he is, in a picture posted by E! News on Instagram, dressed sharply in a dark-blue suit, on the red carpet of the People's Choice Awards. He stands taller now than he did when I met him, but his smile is the same: conspiratorial. I slide my finger through the images and see that while they did not walk the red carpet together, Jack was seen at multiple after-parties canoodling with his *Flames Flicker Eternal* costar Ginny Friedrich. The rumor mill has been churning about their relationship ever since they first appeared together on-screen. Neither has confirmed the nature of their relationship to the press, but based on how regularly they are spotted together, it is safe to assume that they've been happily coupled up for some time now. That this remains the case is a strange comfort to me. It means there's nothing from me to mull, consider, long for, what-if. I turn my screen to black and close my eyes.

VI

Jack

"Right here is good, thanks," I tell the driver as he pulls up to the lot.

I flash my badge at the security guard in the booth, whose tossed-off nod of approval indicates he doesn't notice or care who I am.

I've been on plenty of sets, but it is my first time shooting on a studio lot, and the very idea of it—the old-school energy it conjures—gives me a real thrill. Like I could summon the spirits of Gene Kelly and Donald O'Connor tap dancing in *Singin' in the Rain* or Frank Sinatra and Marlon Brando bantering in *Guys and Dolls*.

Allowing myself to be consumed by this nostalgia is a balm. Knots in my stomach put me off anything for breakfast except a piece of toast and a cup of tea.

Flames Flicker Eternal was a sleeper hit; everyone on production went in knowing it was a small, quiet piece of work made on a shoestring budget. We never expected it to set certain parts of the world on fire. And while the Bone Collector series was a big step for me, I was but one part of the dark superhero-based-on-a-popular-graphic-novel-series ensemble. Since, I'd been the younger version of Colin Firth in a well-liked but little-seen indie and a well-meaning love interest in a romantic comedy wherein American expat Dakota Johnson ultimately chooses herself. I hadn't quite realized until the ink was dry that this particular role would make me a colead in a film with studio backing for the first time; *Gatsby* could determine whether I have "box office bankability." Whether I'm a celebrity with a nice film career or an actor who can have his pick of roles.

Golf carts whip past me. Extras clad in period attire take calls and text during breaks, some productions already hours into shooting for the day. At Building 22 on Lot 1, I steel myself for a second and inhale a breath of warm, dry California air.

"Mind grabbing the door for me there, buddy?" a burly man in a flannel button-down calls out in a deep baritone, hauling a ladder on his shoulder.

I'm blocking the doorway for a gaggle of crew members trying to load in. I fumble for the handle and gesture for them to walk in before me. As I turn to enter after them, I see it: the interior of Gatsby's house. It's a showstopper. Endless intricate details have been constructed for the modern-day take on his living room: impeccably carved floor-to-ceiling windows with art deco varnishing, a matte-gold coffee table, a sprawling C-shaped camel suede couch, and a magnificent Murano glass chandelier descending from the ceiling.

Scores of people mill about, but I hardly notice them.

My original aim of using my extra time on set to take in the broad landscape of this production has narrowed considerably with my urge to study every piece.

I move in for a closer look and gravitate toward the mantel and its rows of Fabergé eggs—a nod to the East and West Egg of Gatsby's world. I hold my breath as I bring my face closer to one of them. It looks too grand to be plastic, like it has a heft to it. With a glance over my left shoulder, then my right, I find that the rest of the crew is too busy rigging the lights and setting up the first shot of the day to be bothered by me nosing around.

I reach toward the egg and am cut off by a sharp "Hey!" A woman is rushing toward me. Average height, with blond hair piled atop her head, wearing pitch-black coveralls and a headset around her neck. My eyes put together the person in front of me like they're assembling a thousand-piece puzzle. The caramel-brown eyes. The slightly upturned nose. The strong arms. Cara.

"Do me a favor?" she asks in a tone that suggests it's not really a question. "Please don't touch the set dressing."

I search her eyes for a flicker of recognition.

"Cara?" Her eyes meet mine with a gaze that reveals nothing. *Does she not remember me?* "What are you doing here?"

"I'm the production designer," she replies simply.

"I thought the production designer was CJ Ericson."

"I *am* CJ Ericson."

I wait for her to say something, anything else that acknowledges a history that predates this very moment.

"Jack. I'm Jack. I'm playing Nick in the movie." The words fall out of my mouth on their own, my brain buzzing too loudly to function properly. "We've met before."

"Yeah, I know," Cara—or *CJ*, rather—says with a laugh. She arches her eyebrow.

"I thought you were Cara . . ." I trail off.

"I only went by Cara at the bar as a ploy."

"A ploy?"

"To see if using a more feminine name got me more tips."

"And?"

"It did," she replies with a shrug.

Her walkie-talkie burbles, and she laughs again. "I usually save my Abbott and Costello routines for after 10 a.m.," she jokes.

"They told me a CJ Ericson was working on the movie, but I didn't know it was you, or . . ." I trail off.

"Or what?" she asks, eyeing me suspiciously, as though I am about to tear a mask off to reveal myself to be something or someone else entirely. "Listen, if this is going to be a problem . . ."

"Oh, God, no. Not a problem at all." I cringe.

"The sets are spectacular," I tell her as I move around the space, an attempt to give myself a few feet of distance to process this turn.

"Thank you." I hear the grin in her voice and look over my shoulder to see it. She's standing still, arms crossed, sizing me up or surveilling me; it's hard to tell which. Witnessing her in her element on set makes seeing her in that bar all those years ago feel, well, like seeing those background actors on the lot in period garb. They were—and she was—out of context. I sense I'm getting a more complete picture now. Her self-possession has a worthy outlet here. She is calm and assured, her posture and stillness projecting a stature betrayed by her actual height. She isn't capitulating to me or working to make me, number two on the call sheet, feel more comfortable. It's the same dynamic she established that night at the bar, and it's having the same effect on me now as it did then.

"Wait until you see the rest of them," she says, dropping her voice slightly and taking a small step toward me. I catch the scent of her, and she smells . . . familiar. Basil and something floral. Lavender, maybe.

"I can't wait," I reply, not bothering to hide my eagerness. "If you have some time later, I'd love to see some of the set specs, or anything else . . ."

Excitement enters CJ's eyes and then vacates so abruptly I think I might have imagined it.

"I need to get home as quickly as I can once I'm wrapped." She looks down for one beat. "For my daughter, Agnes."

There's a bubble in my throat like I swallowed a large rock. "Daughter! Wow." *Christ, you're an actor. Do better.* "How old is she?" In the last five years, she has managed to reinvigorate her career and have a child. I have lost one, two, and, as of a few weeks ago, three People's Choice Awards.

"She's four." There's barely a pause before she continues,

answering the question that's surely registered on my face. "I had Agnes with my ex."

Relief washes over me at the word "ex." "Look, I hope this isn't . . . weird or anything." I pause to search for the right next words but come up short. "Because of how we know each other." *That sounded so much more workplace-appropriate in my head.*

"It's nothing," CJ says as she spots a PA balancing three martini coupes in his hands. "Don't carry the glasses like that! Use the case!" she calls after him.

"Mr. Felgate?" I turn to find a crew member behind me, clutching a clipboard and wearing a T-shirt that reads "*This Is Us* Season 6." "You're early. Do you need help finding your trailer?" I give CJ a wave as I'm led away, and she gives me a distracted nod back.

VII

CJ

So, he does remember me. I flip that knowledge over again and again in my head.

Maybe I'd be less surprised if I hadn't spent the time it took to brew and drink my morning coffee burrowing further down the rabbit hole of his love life. According to WhosDatedWho.com, Jack's had more flings than a rubber band. He's rumored to have dated every single March sister in 2019's *Little Women* and possibly one from the 1994 production too. And that's just the start.

When we met five years ago, he had puppy-dog eyes that couldn't quite believe his good fortune in the industry. Today, those eyes have a few more lines around them, but they still hold wonder in a way that ignites something in me. I've seen people adjust to celebrity overnight and lose their enchantment with Hollywood faster than their checks could clear. He seems to have maintained a firm grasp of his awe.

An hour after my second first encounter with Jack, I stand with the rest of my department waiting for our director, Timmy, to give his big speech before he starts blocking the first scene. Brianna, a prop master I worked with on *The Bee's Knees* and brought on for *Gatsby*, puts her hand over her mouth to stifle a yawn. Getting back into the swing of early call times is tough—maybe even more so when you don't have a kid at home with her own crack-of-dawn production schedule.

My mind loops back to my interaction with Jack, rewinding and playing it again from the beginning. Had he been nervous? It's not that I wasn't, exactly—just that I didn't really see the point of dwelling on it.

It's not like I haven't dabbled in on-set relationships before. But those were clandestine hookups, fueled by forced proximity and the euphoric haziness that comes with making something out of nothing. They were always with someone who was in a different department, who handled a wholly separate part of production, who would have no say as to whether I could be hired on another project. Almost like being a teenager dating someone who went to a different school. Jack, though—he's one of the stars of this film. No one cares if a best boy grip is sneaking off with someone from hair and makeup, but many, many people are invested in the health and happiness of lead actors. The two of us would be as confusing and unlikely as when the basket case and the athlete get together at the end of *The Breakfast Club*.

My brain replays the tape on another memory: one of my earliest gigs as an art department PA on a raunchy, big-budget, R-rated comedy. A woman in makeup made the mistake of hooking up with a comedian who wasn't exactly known for his tact. He told anyone and everyone who would listen, in great detail, what happened between them. At some point, she stopped showing up for work. I shudder at the thought of it and how quickly everyone moved on and she was replaced.

"You OK?" Brianna gently elbows me in the ribs, and I realize that I've been so lost in my own thoughts that I missed Timmy making his entrance, wearing his signature New York Knicks flat-brimmed hat.

"Totally, yes. Mental to-do list," I respond, and Brianna bites her lip anxiously. This film is a big deal for her too, and I feel the weight of that—of wanting to do right by my whole team and to open up doors for them.

"The first time I read *The Great Gatsby*, I wept," Timmy starts from his perch on an apple box. "I was twenty-seven years old. *How* had I never read it before? Well, for one, I paid someone to write my term paper on it in high school. But now I know what I missed: Here we have a story about love, about money, about the American dream. It permeated my consciousness. I knew, then and there, that *I* needed to adapt this film. To do something modern and new but true."

I scan the faces of the hundreds of people who make up the cast and crew. About half are giving earnest nods, newcomers who either think Timmy is a genuine visionary or are overcome with excitement to be on the movie, or both. The other half are industry vets who have been working longer than Timmy has been alive and have learned to mask their disinterest with expressions that read "I'm listening." Their thoughts are more likely on the crafty table, brimming with bags of chips and freshly baked chocolate chip cookies.

I'm standing toward the back of the crowd, but I can still see Jack sitting in his actor's chair. He looks game, making those eager, engaged eyes. The way his foot is hooked on the chair's rung tugs at my memory—it's like I can almost feel the tequila in my stomach and the way he lifted me onto the bar. The mix of confidence and nerves that he wore so well and appears to still.

On either side of him are the actresses playing Jordan Baker and Daisy Buchanan, each of them waifish and compelling in their own way. And then there's Gatsby himself: a strapping, husky, Australian blond named Boone, who manages to make Jack look almost like a pipsqueak. An attractive, charming, British pipsqueak who once went down on me at my place of business and then took me to his hotel after.

Timmy pulls a tattered paperback out of his back jeans pocket and brandishes it for the crowd to see. He has the kind of youthful, long and lean body that suggests an appetite for destruction yet bears none of the markers of excess. "*This* is my copy." Timmy flips through the book for effect, rotating his body so that we can all see. "I've read it countless times. I feel that every character in this book—Gatsby, Nick, Daisy—is an extension of myself. And I think that is why this book has remained so beloved, because these people, in their search for meaning . . . connection . . . success, are *Just. Like. Us.*"

I am not good at drinking the Kool-Aid, but making it in this world requires the ability to give a convincing "Mmm!" while taking the tiniest sips of it possible. It's the professional equivalent of playing tea party with Agnes. I do my best to commit every word of Timmy's monologue to memory so that I can recite it to Stuart later when I relieve him of his babysitting duties. I feel a pang in my heart as I realize he's probably buckling her into a car seat for school right about now. And then I chastise myself for my inability to keep my attention on what's happening in front of me.

"I am so honored that every single one of you has entrusted me to lead you on this journey." Timmy pauses. "I'd like to think that if F. Scott was here, he would approve of what we're doing. But if he didn't . . ." Timmy trails off, appearing to really weigh what F. Scott Fitzgerald might say to him. "Well, the book is in the public domain now."

I surprise myself by joining the scatter of laughs from the crowd. Timmy is brash, overconfident, but at least the tiniest bit self-aware.

"I am so grateful to each of you for trusting me to steer this ship and believing in my vision. And you know what they say: There are no small parts, only small houses on the Northern Shore of Long Island."

"OK, first unit, places in five!" The assistant director calls, and people begin to mill about.

I smile and nod toward Brianna and the rest of my

department, and they look as eager as I am to get down to it. Walking away, I cast a glance over my shoulder and see Jack looking my way. Our eyes lock, and he dips his head ever so slightly in my direction, as though he is tipping his hat to me. He smiles a private smile, and I give him one back.

VIII

Jack

"OK, cut!" Timmy's voice booms from a megaphone behind a row of screens at video village. A week into filming, we're tackling some of the one-on-one scenes between Nick and Gatsby outside his manse. I pull Nick's fake glasses off my face for a moment, blinking and gathering myself as Timmy makes his way toward Boone and me underneath the warm lights. Standing next to Timmy, observing us intently, is CJ.

I've only seen her in passing since our first day of production. Her team is always a few days ahead of the filming schedule, readying the next sets for us. But if her opinion is needed on final set-decorating touches, she sits with Timmy during filming. Like she is today.

I look over at Boone, who's having his face dabbed by a makeup assistant between takes. He's a 6'5" Australian with a well-above-average resting heart rate who subsists on vegemite and bangers, and after a few minutes of filming, he is often dripping sweat. I once attempted a viral video detailing his workout and couldn't make it past the first minute.

Timmy sidles up to us. "Great stuff. I'm loving it."

I brace for whatever note comes next. So far, Timmy's direction has been . . . unorthodox, with instructions like "Try saying your lines like you have a really bad sinus infection."

"Jack," Timmy says, leaning in slightly before dropping his voice to a whisper, "I think you may be overselling it a bit."

I blush, both at his gentle directness and at the realization that I've reverted to the type of just-showy performance I gave when I was greener and doing live theater with friends in the audience. I was attempting to impress them then, and I am attempting to impress CJ now. "Consider it fixed."

"Wait," CJ calls out and holds up a finger before walking up to Timmy to share her thoughts in a low voice I can't quite hear. Whatever she says, Timmy considers it, cocks an eyebrow, and nods his head.

With that, CJ steps toward me briskly, and I take in a gulp of air. My heart climbs into my throat as she comes closer, like she's tugging on it with a chain. Suddenly, she's directly in front of me, her chin tilted up so I can make out each freckle on the bridge of her nose. I turn down to look at her, and I can feel her breath and smell whatever hair products she uses. Her eyes are locked on mine. It's entirely unclear to me what's going to happen next, and it takes all of my will to remember we are *at work*, *on set*, and were I to get hard in this moment, it would be inappropriate at best and maybe an OSHA violation at worst.

"Can I see those for a second?" she asks, gesturing toward my glasses.

I nod and seal my lips, realizing only now they were parted.

CJ reaches for the glasses and gently pulls them from my face, her finger grazing my ear.

She considers them for a moment, round and horn-rimmed. Then, with remarkable conviction, she uses the button on the cuff of her shirt to put a scratch in the lens.

I wince. She grins.

"He's surrounded by all this insane wealth," she says, handing them back to me. "But he's wearing scraped glasses. He can't see things clearly, and he can't afford new ones."

I put the glasses back on my face. She has a point, but I also have no trouble seeing her. The line of her jaw and the collar of her shirt, open at the neck. *Is she warm under the lights, or is she blushing?*

"Brilliant," I say. It's a one-word answer and a full sentence. She goes back behind the monitor, and moments later, we're rolling again.

I take Timmy's direction, but between takes, I steal glances at CJ, curious if I can catch any sort of reaction. Her face is completely impassive; if this were the World Series of Poker championship, she'd bring home the whole pot.

"Cut! We got it!" Timmy claps triumphantly. "We're moving on!" A bell rings, and the crew gets to work prepping for a romantic scene between Daisy and Gatsby.

I stand motionless as everyone scurries around me.

When CJ hurries off for her next agenda item of the day, I chase after her without a specific end goal in mind.

"Hey," I say at her back, a few decibels too loud.

"Hey," she says, stopping short and turning around.

"Thank you for the adjustment back there. It made a difference for me."

"It's my job," CJ says, but she's glowing.

This shirt she's wearing—boxy cut, thick fabric—should distract from her form, but it's having the opposite effect. I am back to thinking of the time I saw her wearing nothing at all, the things we did and said, the way she slipped on *my* shirt to go to the loo after—

I cut these thoughts off at the pass, feeling like I am somehow invading her privacy by accessing my own memories.

She opens her mouth to say something, then pauses, our eyes locked. Color rushes to her cheeks. I know it's not the lights now.

"It was nice to watch filming today and not just the dailies," she says, her voice softer. "The way you're bringing out the deadpan humor in the script is so good. It's very *Metropolitan*."

"My favorite Whit Stillman," I beam, ready to gush.

But before I can, there's a swift energy shift from CJ, and she's back to buttoned-up. "I should get going. I have a meeting with Wardrobe." She sighs out a rush of air, turns, and walks off.

Normally, I'd be in my trailer already. Costume hung, makeup off, with an eye toward plans for the evening if the next morning's call time isn't too early. But I'm not ready to go yet. I want to see how all of the pieces of the production are coming together. I want to see what other changes CJ might make on the fly. I want to see CJ.

Well, there's no rule I have to leave, I think. I follow in her wake.

IX

CJ

As soon as I sit down at the desk in my office, there's a knock at the door. Once, then twice.

"Come in!" I yell, expecting Brianna, who I asked to come give her opinion on a few different furniture options we pulled for Tom's secret city bachelor pad.

Instead, it's Jack.

I stand immediately as he enters, like I've been caught in the act of something other than trying to organize my thoughts and my tasks. I watch his eyes take in the cluttered room, closer to a walk-in closet than a true workspace. There are swatches of paint on the wall so I can see what each looks like after it dries, knee-high piles of paper, props we almost certainly won't need but that I keep around just in case, spare bits of discarded wood, various types of glue. My office is the place for everything the art department chews up and spits out. It's the clutter that I try to keep out of the rest of my life.

"Sorry about the mess," I tell Jack, like this is unusual.

As though I would have tidied if I had known he was coming. I grab a stack of files off the floor and shove them in my desk drawer, the Sisyphean equivalent of using a paper towel to absorb the ocean.

"Please. The mess is what I came for," he says, eyes roving the walls. "Are these your set designs?" He looks at the giant blueprints pinned to the wall, grasping his chin between his thumb and forefinger.

I join him. "They are."

"I know I'm biased"—he glances in my direction now—"but the one you did for Nick's little Long Island shack is especially brilliant. It reminds me of the house from *REDS*—the Croton-on-Hudson one that Jack and Diane have."

This is what made me shut down in the hallway. This callback to our shared cinematic references and the night we established them. But it lands differently behind closed doors. We're still very much at work, but I'm not worried about another member of the crew noticing my heart skip a beat.

"A three-hour movie about communism starring Warren Beatty, Diane Keaton, and Jack Nicholson? Script doctored by Elaine May? *And* it turned a profit? Could never happen today."

"One of the most romantic movies of all time," Jack replies. Our eyes are on the wall, and we're standing at least a foot apart. But I feel his presence warming the entire length of the left side of my body. "The way Beatty did it is the dream," Jack continues quietly. "To have a production company and start projects from the ground up. To be hands-on and only make things I really believe in."

I nod. This is the first I've heard Jack say this, but it feels like information I've sensed all along. Of course he wants to be behind the scenes too. The way he carries himself on set, that he stops and speaks to everyone, that he never asks a PA to drop everything and fetch him a macchiato. He has the nonthreatening charisma of the old-Hollywood actors I'd grown up admiring, Gregory Peck or Robert Redford.

He turns to face me abruptly, arms crossed, one hand on his chin. "Listen, I have a favor to ask you." He clears his throat, and I wish I didn't find his bumbling quite so winning. "This is the biggest role—really, the most authority—I've ever had in a film. And I think—I hope—I can use it to learn as much as possible."

I wait.

"Including production design."

I peer at Jack curiously. He bites his lip, and my eyes rest on his teeth. There are plenty of stars who double as "producers," but those are often vanity credits meant to please difficult egos. I'd heard of actors invested in the experience, who want to know how a film is built from the ground up, but this is my first time meeting one. It feels like encountering a unicorn.

"You can ask me questions," I offer, and I know I sound noncommittal. But I'm worried that letting even a drop of enthusiasm into my voice is leading myself on, opening the door to imagining that this could turn into something more than a classroom experience for him. Maybe it can be like exposure therapy. Spending a little bit of time together to make doing so feel normal, mundane even.

I force myself to say what I've been dwelling on since the first day of filming. "And, you know, whatever happened between us . . . was so long ago now." I get the words out as fast as I can. "If you could do me the favor of not mentioning it to anyone."

"Absolutely, of course not," Jack says just as quickly, as if to beat the idea away with a stick.

I pull what I have to say next from deep within the recesses of my stomach. I owe it to him and to myself. "I should tell you . . . we met that night . . . under very different circumstances." The words catch on their way out. "I didn't want to say anything at the time, but my mom was . . . really sick." I force myself to speak about this as vaguely as possible so that I don't summon each painful memory of the time.

Jack's eyes crinkle, and his jaw slackens as he takes in this information and leans his body slightly toward me. I need to keep talking so he can't say "I'm so sorry" because I can't stand to hear this from one more person, and especially not him. "She died not long after we met. But that night— it was sort of a bright spot during a very tough time. So, I just wanted you to know that. To thank you for that."

He takes his time before responding, and his obvious comfort with the silence between us feels almost alarmingly intimate. "I'm glad . . . that I could . . . be there for you," Jack replies, seemingly cutting and pasting his words together from a longer draft in his head. He uncrosses his arms and lifts his hand, like he might reach for me.

"I'm happy to help you, if I can," I say, eyes on his palm. "Ask me any questions you want about production design. Please don't hesitate." My abrupt transition to this cordial, professional tone makes me feel like I'm fleeing the scene of a crime. But it's not like I could stay there either.

Jack takes it in stride. "That would be brilliant. Thank you."

I reach for his hand and give it a nice, firm shake. *This will feel normal soon*, I think. *Any second now, this will feel normal.*

X

Jack

"Hands down, the best place to eavesdrop," CJ announces a few days later as we pull up chairs at a metal, circular table next to a well-trafficked coffee cart on the lot. She tilts her head toward two nearby suits having a seemingly tense conversation. One of them grips an empty coffee cup tightly.

"What do you think they're talking about?" I ask.

She squints her wide eyes like she's trying to focus. The words "condensing" and "fourth-quarter revenue" and "drama library" waft toward our table.

"I think we're witnessing the birth of a new streaming service bundle."

I pretend to check my calendar on my phone. "Sadly, I don't think I'll be able to attend the christening."

CJ *tsk*s at me. "But you'll send a gift."

"I'll have my people call their people," I joke.

"Quick, say you're starring in *Avatar 4*, and see how long it takes to leak to the trades."

I laugh and watch her take a sip of the iced coffee she

wouldn't let me pay for. My eyes rest on her lips, and I force myself to look away, up at the cloudless sky.

"So, your questions?"

I would've been happy to go back and forth, enjoying our dip into an ease that we haven't quite found since *Gatsby* started. I almost forget this conversation has a stated purpose, one that I proposed.

"Right." I clear my throat, and her eyes brighten. "Earlier, I heard you talking with the DP, and you said you wanted him to get more wide shots. How come?"

CJ places her coffee down purposefully. A pool of condensation gathers underneath it.

"Two reasons," she starts, ready, willing, and able to defend any decision she makes or directive she gives. "First, to see the elements the team designed in one frame. To get the full effect. Second, from a story perspective, we talked a lot about how much of the frame Gatsby and Daisy would take up. But we designed the sets so that both Gatsby and Daisy would be basically dwarfed by their homes and the wealth that surrounds them, the thing that they're both powerless against."

I can't help myself. "That *you* designed. You did that."

"All of this is a group effort."

"No one is here. You're allowed to take credit," I tease.

She relents and sips her drink. "OK, yes, the sets *I* designed. But you never know what one detail people are going to love or fixate on for years, and it can come from anyone: the director, the star, the prop master, a PA."

CJ's phone buzzes, and she flips it over, her lips shifting into a wistful smile as she reads a message.

"Is everything OK?" I ask.

"My daughter's school has this thing where each letter in the alphabet gets a day, and each kid gets assigned a letter. 'B' is today, and it's Agnes's letter. She wanted me to buy her a shirt with a giant bee on it, but I convinced her to make one with me instead. Her only condition was that we use lots of glitter. Her grandfather just sent a picture of her in it."

"Sounds very cute." I want to ask to see, but I don't know what's appropriate.

She turns her eyes to me, weighing something, then flips her phone toward me too. Agnes is visibly CJ's daughter: the playground-wild version of her hair and upturned nose, but with a rounder face and missing her brown eyes. She's smiling like she's found a golden ticket, and I can see the arm of the person snapping the photo.

"That's sweet of your dad to take her to school when you're on set."

"Oh, Stuart is not—well, he's kind of my dad."

I can feel the confusion register on my face.

"OK, so he is my dad, but I didn't know he was my biological father until I was a teenager. He's gay but was in more of an . . . experimental phase when he and my mom first knew each other. He traveled a lot when I was growing up, so my mom thought it'd be easier to sort of pass him off as my fun Uncle Stuart instead of a dad figure, so it's been hard to see him as my actual father as a result. Even after . . . everything that happened with my mom. And how much he helps me with Agnes."

"Is Agnes's father, does he . . ." I start to ask, attempting to choose my words carefully and falling short.

"She's with him some weekends." She pauses and sits up straighter. "Having her was very much my decision . . . on my own. He wasn't ready to sign up for fatherhood, and I knew that. And he works on film sets, too, and travels a ton. We met through mutual work friends."

"That must be a lot, single parenting."

"I got pregnant a little while after my mom died. It wasn't on purpose, but after all of this loss and grief, it felt like something new, something right. My life had already completely imploded, and I figured, if I ever wanted a baby, why not now? You know, you always think, *I'll be ready when I'm older* or *It isn't a good time.* But when is there really a perfect time for anything?"

I nod, probably too emphatically, in an effort to encourage her to keep answering questions I wouldn't dare ask.

"Plus, all those years of seeing my mom doing it by herself made me think that I could do it too. It feels like . . . a way of honoring her somehow."

"I'm sure she would be enormously proud of you. Of all you're doing," I say quietly.

She smiles a little at this and looks lost in thought. Her right hand, with an emerald band on her middle finger, rests across from mine on the table. The urge to take it in my own comes over me; I move both my hands to my lap to ensure I don't.

"At the very least, she would absolutely get a kick out of seeing Stuart snap into action as a family man," CJ replies after a moment, whatever thought she was lost in shipped back to the edges of her mind. "Although I swear any night now, I'm going to come home and catch him showing her one of the wildly inappropriate experimental films he made when he was younger."

"He's a filmmaker?"

"Some obscure stuff, but he had a few cult hits in the '90s. He likes to say he would've been John Waters if John Waters wasn't John Waters."

A bell goes off in my head. "Wait, you're not talking about Stuart Blitz, are you?"

She looks at me like I've won *Countdown*. "You know Stuart Blitz?"

"I got my hands on a VHS of *Wheels of Steel* when I was in high school, and I wore it out watching it so much. I thought the motorcycle gang was the coolest thing on the planet. You should have seen the leather jacket I wore around during that phase."

"I can't believe you're a big fan of Stuart's. I thought that was reserved for friends and family only." Her phone buzzes again, this time with an alarm. "OK, well, I have a meeting with Timmy, but let's do this again."

I take comfort even as she walks away, well aware now that she wouldn't say it if she didn't mean it.

XI

Jack

"I watched *How to Steal a Million* last night," I announce to CJ as I stride up alongside her after arriving early to the lot one evening the following week. She's standing in front of a set as art PAs mill about.

"Oh yeah?" She doesn't turn to look at me, but I can see her eyes flash with excitement. Two days prior, she'd rattled off a list of movies I needed to watch to rectify my "honestly shameful" knowledge gap around Audrey Hepburn. I'd tapped the assignment into a note I keep on my phone titled "CJ" that's mostly littered with questions I want to ask her.

Around us, crew members are prepping Gatsby's living room for an overnight shoot. What was once an immaculate, practically gleaming apartment is now covered in detritus left over from one of Gatsby's parties. Signs warn that it's a hot set, meaning: The trash is intentional. CJ and Brianna monitor the progress. We're now nearly two weeks into filming, and staying on schedule is paramount.

"You know, when I was a kid," CJ starts. She still has

eyes on the set, but she shifts closer to me. "I thought that Audrey played the same character in every movie. Like an Audrey Hepburn Cinematic Universe."

"A-H-C-U. Sounds close to 'achoo,' but we can work with it," I say, going for a joke.

CJ tries to mask a grin, but I don't hide mine. Her eyes move across the space, and I follow them to find Timmy heading toward us. Missing from the top of his head is his Knicks hat, which is clutched tightly in his hands. I've never seen him without it before. He has a strained, anxious look on his face.

"Give me a second," she tells me as she steps away to meet him.

I watch the pair exchange words in my peripheral vision. Or, rather, I watch as Timmy tells CJ what's plaguing him, and she nods thoughtfully, jumping in with a reaction here and there. After a few minutes, she grabs her walkie.

Almost immediately, a PA materializes at my side, ushering me to my trailer, and I follow begrudgingly. I want to stay and witness CJ at work. My brain tingles pleasantly at the prospect of watching her solve a particularly vexing puzzle, and I realize that were we ever in any kind of danger, I'd risk being too turned on watching her swing into action to be much help at all.

When I reemerge, summoned at last, we aren't at Gatsby's house: We are at a replica of Bemelmans, the famed Carlyle Hotel bar in New York. An earlier scene between Daisy and Jordan—one that wasn't in the book or any of the other film versions—was set there, but I'm not sure what we're doing back again. Because the crew had already started breaking it down, they'd taken the last few hours to rebuild it, which means the shot list had to be thrown out and rewritten, which means we are in for an even later night than planned.

In scenarios like this, an actor can go one of two ways: Ask a slew of questions and slow things down further, or zip it and roll with it. It's door number two for me. Whatever the explanation, I know CJ worked painstakingly to duplicate the bar, and this, if anything, is another chance to showcase it.

"Sorry about the last-minute change," Timmy mumbles when Boone and I take our places alongside extras filling out the milieu. There's no time for rehearsal; we will have to wing it. "Are we ready to rock?"

I look over at CJ, sitting behind the monitor next to Timmy. Her face is fixed with concentration. She's told me over coffee how much she hates these last-minute changes, when attention to detail gets discarded, but I'd never know it by observing her. She appears calm, poised, and ready to get to work. Nothing on her face suggests exhaustion, even though it's now 11 p.m. and she is staring down the barrel of a twelve-hour shift.

"Rolling," I hear.

"The first time I saw her, we were only seventeen years old," Boone says, a rueful Gatsby. "She was the most beautiful thing I'd ever seen in my life." He looks away from me, down at the bar.

I open my mouth, but Timmy jumps in before I can get my line out.

"Cut! They should be drinking something. It doesn't make sense that they'd be at a bar and not drinking." He turns to CJ. "Can we have glasses and prop liquor?"

"The ones we used for the other bar scene are in storage now."

"We can use whatever we have around. Brianna, grab the closest glasses and bring them over."

"Timmy, let us get the right ones," CJ says calmly.

"You really think anyone cares about what glasses they drink from?"

"Respectfully, they do. Otherwise I wouldn't have a job."

Everyone on the crew is watching, waiting to see if this will morph into a full-blown argument or remain a skirmish. There isn't a trace of anger—or any emotion—in CJ's voice. She's confident and assured. Neither loud nor quiet, neither timid nor condescending. The same way she managed those fans the first night we met.

I've never seen anyone up close with so much conviction in my entire life. I am both turned on and ready to follow her into war.

"We need to get filming. We don't have time to get the other glasses," Timmy insists.

"If Brianna takes the golf cart, she'll be back with the glasses in twenty minutes. The more time we spend talking about it, the longer it'll delay her."

"We don't have twenty minutes."

"If we've been waiting this long, another twenty minutes isn't going to make or break anything. Would you rather wait twenty minutes to get the glasses we sourced for the bar or look at your film, know that this detail is off, and know that it will be discussed and dissected online?"

Timmy sighs and returns the Knicks cap to his head. "Brianna, go get the glasses." And with that, she's off.

I've seen countless crew members and producers capitulate to the director and many productions that were all the worse for it. I search CJ's face for evidence that she knows what a big deal it is that she stood her ground and came out victorious. I make out the tiniest trace of a smile but only because I'm beginning to learn exactly what to look for.

XII

CJ

I'm back in my office after we have finally—*finally*—wrapped for the evening, and I need to get home to sleep before I'm back here tomorrow afternoon. I should be exhausted by the sheer number of hours we put in today, but I'm still coming down from the adrenaline spike of sparring with Timmy in front of the cast and crew. I kept my cool during our standoff—Brianna assured me, and I trust her to give it to me straight—but in the aftermath, my body is buzzing. Here in my little space, I'm able to process that I'm proud of myself. And not just for holding my own, but for knowing when to do it. I've learned from observing my bosses over the years to pick and choose your battles. And if you're going to pick one, pick one you can win.

I look out at the piles and piles of stuff in my office and wonder if I'm better off crashing here, since Stuart is sleeping at the house and Agnes will be up making noise in a matter of hours.

A knock at the door interrupts my deliberation. At my "Yeah?" Jack steps through the frame, still in costume.

"Is everything OK?" I scan his form, looking for signs we're being called back to set. That Timmy wants to shoot with those random bottle-green highball glasses after all. I can't think of a reason why Jack isn't already in a car home by now. But he looks wide awake, and when he flashes a smile, it's like he's got a secret to tell me.

"I just wanted to say . . . I thought you were really brilliant tonight."

I blush at the compliment but brush it off, urging my cheeks to calm. "Oh please, that was nothing." I don't mean it.

"Oh, come on. Hardly any of us would've stood up to Timmy in that moment. I mean, I don't think I would've. I was . . ." His eyes fall to his shoes. "Hey, would you want to get a drink?"

At this, the adrenaline that is already coursing through me finds a way to spike even higher. We're at work. The temptation is colossal, and against the backdrop of all the coffee breaks Jack and I have shared over the last week and change, my brain starts to apply a murky logic and build its case: Those lattes were drinks, weren't they? *No*, I have to shut it down. I'm tired, sitting here in front of a man who I find impossibly charming and talented and attractive—"impossibly" being the key word. The answer is obviously no.

"It's after midnight in Los Angeles. Practically nothing's open," I say instead.

Jack reaches into Nick Carraway's jacket without breaking eye contact and pulls out a bottle of Espolòn.

"Have you ever been to the Carlyle?" Jack asks me, settling into the seat at the faux Bemelmans that Boone occupied only an hour before.

"A few times to scout for this project. Right around when preproduction started, a theater in New York was doing a retrospective on Stuart's films, so he, Agnes, and I flew out for it. But I haven't spent much time in New York otherwise."

"You haven't?"

"What? Is that surprising?"

"I don't know. There's something worldly about you."

"By worldly . . . do you mean old?"

Jack laughs. "I'm fairly certain we're the same age." It's true; FamousBirthdays.com confirmed for me that Jack is thirty-four too.

I take a sip of the tequila we mixed with Sprite from the vending machine. I feel his eyes on my throat as I swallow.

He shifts his body toward me and rests his elbow on the bar. "I think I mean you're . . . wise and grounded."

"Maybe just compared to the people you know."

He chuckles and makes a face feigning insult. "Fair point there." He raises his glass toward me and holds my eyes. I don't look away despite a sense that I should. I know the steps to this dance, and it's starting to feel easier to repeat them than to learn a new one. *Go home*, half of my brain says.

But, the other half of my brain is at the wheel. "I've really only lived in or near LA."

"You never wanted to leave? Try somewhere else?"

I shrug, both at him and at myself. "For most people, it takes so much courage to move to LA. Like, you have to hop off a plane and prove yourself immediately. Being from here and knowing how this city operates, how to get around, how to make it work for you, it almost feels like a superpower."

"I don't even know how to drive." He blurts it out like a confession.

I laugh. "There are solutions to that, you know." I rest my elbow on the bar too and my chin on my hand.

"Right, right. I've never really needed to learn though. In London, I have the Tube, and I'm never anywhere else long enough for it to matter. I don't even have my flat anymore," Jack says as though it's only occurring to him now.

"You don't? How come?"

"Initially, it was to save money—silly if I was barely there anyway—and then, well, with money no longer an issue"—his cheeks redden—"it became easier to stay in the places my team books for me. But I still consider London my home base. Even without a proper home there."

"Why's that?"

"I don't know. London still feels more . . . like a real city to me. With real people. Normal."

"First off," I start, brandishing my pointer finger. The tequila has found its way into my bloodstream and activated my gesticulation muscles. "All cities are real cities, with real people." Jack smirks, like he's satisfied to have provoked such a passionate response. "Secondly, you don't seem like someone who's looking for a normal life."

"What do you mean?" Jack seems genuinely surprised by this.

"Jack. You're a movie star. Have you noticed? You're always out at a party or being paparazzied on a date with Ginny Friedrich." *Dammit, that last bit.* The filter I apply—especially around him—has called it a night.

"That's not what you think."

I raise a brow.

Jack sighs, nods. "OK. We were together, off and on, when we were filming, but it's long over. We just sort of . . . put it on for appearances."

"Why would you do that?"

"Because there's so much competition. Always a hot new star for people to obsess about, and studios want actors who people are talking about. Being spotted at these events . . . especially with Ginny . . . was an easy way to stay top of mind. It feels like making movies is only half the job now that I absolutely refuse to get an Instagram, no matter how much Delia pressures me, but falling into a routine with Ginny felt like an easier assignment. It's a way I could feed the beast without losing myself completely."

"And all the other women you've been spotted with?" I may as well get the questions borne of my internet stalking out now before morning light and sobriety close whatever door we've opened. "The actresses, the influencers, the pop stars," I rattle off, trying to play it like I'm razzing him.

"There have been no influencers!" He clutches his chest. "Some of that . . . might be what you think." Jack looks down at the bar and knocks one of his knees against mine. *Shots fired.* "But some of it is just finding someone I know I can chat with at an event. Do you know how stale those things are? I'm not going to issue a correction or clarification every time someone with an iPhone catches me at a restaurant or chatting at an after-party."

"That . . . makes sense," I say slowly.

"I feel like it took me so long to get here. I don't want to become a victim of it, but I don't want to lose it either," Jack says into his glass, like he doesn't want to voice his insecurity directly to me.

"You won't," I reply with urgency. Sitting at the fake bar, our bodies are angled toward each other, my knee now pressing back against his with an affected casualness as artificial as our surroundings. "You're really good." The spot inside of my knee where our bodies are touching feels electrified, and the tingling current extends upward to my inner thigh, creating a dampness between my legs that feels hard to ignore.

"Yeah, well, it's been ten years, and I still don't feel like I understand this business at all."

"Honestly, I think everyone feels that way."

"Even you?"

My brows shoot up. "Especially me."

"Then you hide it well."

"I hide lots of things well," I say with a shrug, but I know what I'm doing: I want Jack to know I want him, without having to acknowledge that in any real way. I want to get to sit here and flirt with him and have a too-late drink answering too-personal questions while still technically playing by the rules I made for myself.

Jack's gaze darts from my eyes to my lips and back again, like he knows better than to say anything out loud. I set my glass down on the bar, and he sees that as the yes it is.

He angles his torso forward and presses his mouth to mine, his hand reaching for the back of my neck, his thumb brushing back and forth against my earlobe. After all of these years of imagining what it would be like to be with him again, kissing him feels like finding something that I was sure I'd lost forever. My nerves prickle, hyper-aware of every sensation: the sugary soda on his tongue, the unlikely familiarity of the scent of tequila on his breath, the squeeze of my eyes as I try to experience this and only this, the brace of his leg as I lean in closer and he presses his warm palm into my upper thigh.

Jack's other hand winds into my hair, and his mouth seeks out my ear and then my collarbone. I tilt my head to the side and peel my eyes open, and I see, suddenly, in sharp focus all around me the literal, physical evidence of everything I've built and worked toward.

What am I doing? Kissing this actor in the middle of the night?

If anyone we work with finds out about this, no one will take me seriously for the rest of the shoot. I'll be that pro-duction designer who had a fling with one of the stars—on set, no less—and that reputation will follow for who knows how long. This might be the last biggest thing I ever do.

I tense as I spiral, and Jack feels me stiffen before I can get any words out.

"Hey, what's wrong?" he asks, pulling his mouth away, keeping his hands on me.

"Jack, I'm sorry. I can't do this." My eyes sting, and tears threaten. *I am not going to cry over* this.

His puppy-dog eyes are back, shining at me. Pleading.

"I'll see you tomorrow," I say as dispassionately as I can manage, standing up and clearing our glasses. I have to get out of here before I let this go any further.

When I look up at him, still frozen in his seat, I want to ignore the confusion in his features and what appears to be sadness mixed in too. "I really am sorry," I say in an almost whisper, to myself as much as him, before kissing him gently on his cheekbone and briskly walking off the set.

XIII

CJ

The first time I wake up, it's at my desk with a splitting headache, my contact lenses adhered to my eyes, and a call sheet from last week stuck to my cheek. It's been two hours since I put my head down after abandoning Jack at the bar, promising myself I'd only close my eyes for just a few minutes until I felt steady enough to go home.

The second time I wake up, it's in my bed, and it's around noon. My brain feels fuzzy, like it can't quite piece together its journey from the set to my office to a Lyft to my mattress at these off-kilter hours. *When did I last eat something?*

Thoughts of hunger are squashed by the memory of Jack's face when I left him. It wasn't the disappointment of a man used to getting what he wants and confused that he isn't. It was the disappointment of a man whose heart was in it.

I press the side of my face into my pillow as I return to the kiss. It was exactly as I hoped it would be if we ever had the chance again: tender but determined; exciting but reassuring. Of *course* I want more of it, more of him. But for the first time in years, I feel like I've regained control of my life. My career is on track, Agnes is out of the wily toddler years, and I can start making plans for myself that involve more than putting one foot in front of the other. None of those plans can coexist with fucking around with an actor who could derail all of that with the same ease with which he delivers a monologue.

Even as I make this case to myself, I wince. Jack has never been "an actor" to me, not since the first time I met him. *Maybe I shouldn't have left*, I think before I can beat the sentiment back. We could have talked, at least. I could have told him why I can't have an on-set hookup—that it's different for him than for me. And that anything more than that . . . well, what's even the point of thinking that way? To allow myself to fantasize about some sort of relationship with an on-the-rise movie star, who is in such an alternate reality, he doesn't have a permanent address.

I reach for my phone on the nightstand and see forty-seven texts. My throat tightens, and I sit bolt upright in bed. Like I've been caught—and punished—for sleeping during waking hours.

Once I scan the senders—not Agnes's school or Stuart—my heart rate drops to its normal pace. The *Gatsby* art department group chat is blowing up.

"If you wear your costume out to a party, you should have to thank the wardrobe department by name during any acceptance speeches," one of the texts reads.

"Donna is going to have to steam and press that tomorrow, huh," says another.

I scroll up farther. Fuck. Are they talking about *Jack*?

Do they somehow know about what happened between us last night? And how? *Well, there goes any ounce of respectability I once had.*

When I reach the first text from the series, I see this has nothing to do with me: Jack was spotted at an after-after-hours party at some actor's house wearing the Nick Carraway costume he'd been in when I left him. It's a blazer and jeans; not something that would register for anyone who isn't part of the crew of this movie, but for this group, it's front-page news. One of his friends had snapped a selfie that captured Jack and Ginny Friedrich in the background as she whispered something in his ear. A gossip blog published a screenshot of the photo, and social media gossip accounts ran with it. A member of my crew saw it, dropped into this group chat, and delivered it to me in my bed, whether I want it here or not.

The part of me that blossomed in Jack's company wilts instantly. I stare at the picture, giving it a chance to imprint on my brain. Seeing this rewrites my memory of last night: Jack had been after a hookup, and he found it with someone else. I was naive—silly—to read anything more into it, to think that we might need to have A Conversation about anything that doesn't involve props. I feel the urge to compare myself to Ginny—her high-set cheekbones and the kind of perfect complexion attained only via blood relation to British nobility. *What do they even have to talk about?* I wonder, then remember a lot of relationships are not predicated on the need to talk and that I don't know anything about her personality or interests.

I open Instagram, ready to show myself all the ways that Ginny is perfect for Jack, then just as quickly flick the app away. *Ginny is professionally attractive*, I remind myself. And I have a life I feel great about when I'm not minutes removed from a terrible night's sleep and hours removed from a misguided kiss with the one man who has burrowed deep in my consciousness for years.

I need to adjust accordingly. From now on, no more shadowing me, no more asking me set-design questions, no more volleying back and forth film recommendations. I'll keep my distance for the remainder of the shoot. And by now, we're more than halfway through.

XIV

Jack

As I stand over the remnants of three long trays of deli sandwiches, I feel eyes on me. I'm late to set, and this is what I get—the punishment of trying to make a meal of the bits of crust and odds and ends that no one wanted.

I wave at Brianna as she hustles by, and she gives me a sly smirk back. It's enough to make me check that my fly is zipped. Why is everyone looking at me like they've read my diary?

I grab a PA—Manny—and ask something I never do. "Hey, I'm sorry to be a bother, but would you be able to get me a cup of tea?"

Manny nods, head bobbing like he can't stop it. "I'll have that for you right away."

"And, can I ask you a question?" *Am I really going to unleash my paranoia on this poor guy?*

Manny nods again.

"Is there . . . something going on today?"

Manny looks at me quizzically. "I'm not sure what you mean."

I'm underslept and overtired. I don't have the energy to give this conversation a practiced British obtuseness. "I know I probably sound like a silly actor . . . but I get this sense that everyone is looking at me."

Manny glances to his left, then his right. I can tell he's running over what to say in his head. After about thirty seconds of this, I realize I've put him in the uncomfortable position of having to tell an actor the very thing an actor never wants to hear: the truth.

Manny reaches into his pocket, pulls out his phone, taps a few buttons, and hands it to me.

"Hot Stuff! Actor Jack Felgate Cozies Up to Star Girlfriend Ginny Friedrich." An *Us Weekly* headline. Underneath, a zoomed-in, pixelated picture of Ginny next to me, and me still in my Nick Carraway costume like, well, a fucking wanker. I'd been too antsy about asking CJ for a drink to change out of it after we shot, then too disappointed and distracted to take it off after.

"You hadn't seen this yet?" Manny asks, skepticism crossing his face.

"No, I haven't . . . but everyone else has?"

Manny nods, smaller this time, looking fearful that I might take this news out on him. I hand him his phone back.

"Uh, thank you."

"Right back with that cup of tea."

Add this to the growing list of the ways I fucked up over the last twelve hours. I didn't mean to upset CJ, I didn't mean to compound my own agony by going to a party I knew would only make things worse, and I didn't mean to disrespect Wardrobe, which needs that costume back for washing and pressing. That costume that is currently crumpled up in a ball next to the shower in the house I'm renting. I have to go to them and apologize profusely and arrange for a messenger when what I want to do is hide out in my trailer.

Then, I see CJ, clipboard in hand, in a ribbed T-shirt and a pair of jeans, an outfit too much like the one she wore the first time I met her for me to bear in my state. My heart soars at the sight of her, then nosedives when her eyes brush right over me as she continues on her path toward Brianna.

If everyone saw the picture of me with Ginny, CJ saw. Well, fuck. What I told her about Ginny last night is all true, but it's the easy version, and I want CJ to have the full picture of me. So that if she chooses to write me off, at least I've fully earned it.

CJ and Brianna have their heads together when I approach. "CJ, a word?"

"Yes, Jack?" Her brows are lowered, and Brianna looks surprised by her tone. CJ sighs and blinks her eyes a few times.

"May I borrow you for a minute?"

She passes the clipboard to Brianna and starts off toward her office. I follow in silence. At the door, she spins on me, like she's waited exactly as long as she can.

"What is it, Jack?"

I rush to close the distance between us. I reach around her to open the door, knowing she'll regret even the chance that someone could have witnessed this conversation. My head goes light at our proximity: her back against the door; my arm inches from her waist. We step inside, and CJ shuts us in, but we don't move to sit.

"I'm so sorry about last night," I say, instantly regretting my vagueness.

"Clearly you got what you were looking for."

It takes me a second to understand what she means. *What was it that I was looking for?*

Then it dawns on me. "You think all of this has been— you think I was chasing after a shag or something?"

CJ throws her hands in the air. "What else am I supposed to think?"

I take a deep breath. *Tell her.* "I thought it was obvious because I'm not good at hiding these things—and before you mock me, 'you're an actor,' all that, believe me, I know. But I'm going to be direct. I fancy you. I did when I met you, which I know also sounds silly, but I really do now. Even more. And I can't help that we both happen to be working on this movie, which I know makes it seem both complicated and like a bad idea, but I'm really glad we are because otherwise I don't know if we would have ever found each other again. And the more we work together, the more I get to know you, the more interested in you I am."

CJ looks at me stone-faced, only her eyes moving, scanning me. As though she's performing some sort of analysis to determine my intentions.

"Sorry, it's kind of hard to take you seriously when you

say words like 'fancy,'" she says, and I realize I have been holding my breath.

She leans against her desk, her arms crossed; I rest my hand against a storage tower.

"I assume you saw the picture. Of me with Ginny last night."

She crosses her arms tighter. *Don't be bumbling*, I tell myself.

"On-screen, Ginny and I have amazing chemistry."

She cringes, and I hold up a hand.

"Off-screen, there's nothing. No spark. We tried—really tried—to make a go of it, both because we do enjoy each other's company and because we knew it would be good for our careers. I'm embarrassed to say that I really considered just accepting that—a sort of long-term platonic, performative relationship that might have helped get me other things I've been working so hard for. And I know other people in this industry do it." *God, I'm rambling.* "But I realized that's the line for me: that I'll show up for all the parties and be spotted reading a popular novel so I can get cast in the adaptation. That I'll work back-to-back projects and live out of a suitcase. But I won't settle for a 'marriage of convenience,' or whatever kind of thing you would read about in Jane Austen. And Ginny and I—we've talked about this. She has a great childhood love, and I don't know what she'll ever do about that. But she also knows what it's supposed to feel like and that we don't have it, is the point."

CJ drops her arms to her sides, and I take that as a sign to continue.

"At the risk of sounding drippy, I'll say one more thing: That night with you at Swan Dive . . . something clicked for me. It was perhaps the start of me realizing that I was unwilling to just settle into a nice, cozy PR relationship. Even with a person I consider a close friend."

CJ squares her shoulders and inhales a deep breath. "You know, for you, who you date is basically part of the job, but it's not for me. I've seen some pretty nasty stuff on sets before when crew members have gotten mixed up with actors. The actors bragging about it and making women on the crew out to be easy targets."

I shake my head. "Awful," I say and then pause, giving CJ the chance to continue, forgetting she's not as long-winded as me.

"Look," I say, taking a step toward her. "Whatever happens between us, I need you to know, I would never, *ever* let it affect you professionally. I swear on my life, my mum's life, my dad's life, my brother's life, the lives of both Liam and Noel Gallagher, who as an Englishman, I assure you, are very important to me."

At this, CJ fights a smile.

Without saying a word, she closes the space between us, grabs the back of my neck, and kisses me. Like she needs me. Like she won or lost a battle with herself. I can't tell. She pulls away just as quickly, but she keeps her hand on me, and I rest mine on the small of her back, feeling the material of her shirt against my fingertips, her skin underneath it.

"We still work together. It's not really up to you if it affects me professionally . . ." CJ trails off, and I watch her, unaccustomed to her not knowing exactly what she's going to say. She rests her forehead on my cheek. "I like you, Jack, I really do. I sort of hate how much I do. But I can't be part of your world."

"Aren't we part of the same world?"

"My life is quiet. I don't want to be referred to as a 'Mystery Blond' on DeuxMoi because you and I went to dinner at Horses. And I can't risk Agnes's privacy."

I can picture the headline as she says it, the angry comments insinuating I "betrayed" Ginny or that CJ "stole" me. I can't blame her for not wanting to thrust herself—or her kid—into the spotlight.

"The thing is"—I look at her, pleading—"it's not as hard to avoid the cameras as Ben Affleck would have you believe. Listen, after the movie wraps, will you give me a chance? A date somewhere not on the TMZ bus tour route?"

She nods and smiles sheepishly, and as she begins to turn away, my hand goes to her wrist, pulling her into my chest. She tilts her face upward toward mine. "*Jack*," she whispers. "Fourteen days."

"It's nothing, practically nothing," I reply, doing some of the worst acting of my entire life.

XV

CJ

"No *Umbrellas of Cherbourg* tonight, OK?" I chide Stuart, Agnes wrapped around my legs in her favorite polka-dot pajamas.

He laughs. "I've already got *The Muppet Movie* queued up." He kisses me on both cheeks. "Go. You look splendid."

"You look *splendid*," Agnes mimics, and I laugh, giving her dramatic cheek kisses as I unwind her from my bare shins. I'm wearing a navy minidress I acquired from a vintage dealer who works almost exclusively with stylists and costumers, a perk of industry connections. My hair, restricted to a topknot for the last however many weeks, is down, and the sensation of the waves against my bare shoulders heightens my corporeal awareness in a way that's entirely unnecessary tonight.

This evening is the wrap party for *Gatsby*. When you're in the middle of filming a movie, time stretches out before you in a way that makes it hard to imagine that you'll ever work on anything else, that you won't be on this set for the rest of your life. You're in a bubble, like kids away at summer camp. But eventually, it does end, and everyone returns to their lives.

In my case, I will also return to a one-night stand from five years ago.

I step out of the Uber and immediately sense that the wrap party for Timmy Gray's *Gatsby* production is the real deal. These things run the gamut, from a couple of bottles of liquor and a grocery cheese tray cracked open as soon as the director yells "Cut!" for the final time, to tonight's affair: an open bar at a hot new spot in West Hollywood, with paparazzi stationed outside during all hours of operation. As I make my way in, I notice the things Timmy splurged on—wine from Long Island vineyards, oysters from Oyster Bay, and cocktails featuring green absinthe. As my eyes adjust to the dim lighting, I scan for Jack. It dawns on me I haven't seen him off the studio lot since the film went into production. My nerves take hold.

I'd told Jack we needed to keep our distance on set because the temptation to share a look, brush up against each other, or worse had loomed since the moment we'd reencountered one another, and with our mutual attraction made explicit, mere proximity threatened any self-restraint. Once, after a particularly stirring scene where Nick learns the truth about Gatsby's past, I'd rushed over to congratulate him, and without realizing it, I'd found my hand on the hem of his wool sweater, my lower lip clenched between my teeth. He told me he "liked when I watched," and I'd nearly unbuckled his belt right there. The sound of a crew member taking a phone call nearby reminded me of where we were. No one saw us, but it was too close for comfort.

After that, we decided to limit our interactions to texting, and that line of communication quickly turned into a steady stream of flirtation. We'd queue up movies at the same time after our days ended, taking turns choosing the feature presentation: *Hot Fuzz* and *Shaun of the Dead* for him, *Heartburn* and *Mermaids* for me.

Five years, one hookup, two on-set kisses, and now two weeks of texting, and I am uncharacteristically smitten. It's undeniable. And I'm slightly terrified by how unlike me it feels to carry on this way. *What if this thing with Jack was only good for the chase? What if we've built it up so much it can't possibly deliver?* The press of a hand on my lower back interrupts my catastrophizing. The sensation of Jack's breath on my skin accompanies the whispered sound of his voice: "Ready to go whenever you are."

Immediately, my brain and my body are vibrating. I whip my head around to find him standing next to me but staring straight ahead at the bar. He's wearing a gray knit polo I want to pull off over his head. He smiles politely at the bartender and holds up two fingers. "Two Clase Azul on the rocks, please."

I open my mouth to speak, ready to tell him we can leave *right now, actually,* when I catch sight of Brianna and the rest of the department over his shoulder. If we make our escape, we'll miss the chance to celebrate what we all created together.

"One hour," I tell him while mirroring his straight-ahead gaze, like we're two spies arranging an illicit rendezvous.

I can make out the corner of his mouth quirking up.

"Everyone, thanks for being here!" Timmy is on a microphone, the source of his powers, his Knicks hat, affixed firmly on his head. We all shift our attention toward him for what will be the last time.

"I wanted to say thank you all for your hard work. I've believed in this movie ever since I had the idea to make it." He chuckles, and we join him, now better acquainted with his particular brand of nepo-baby humor.

Jack lifts his arms to clap for Timmy, and when he drops them to his sides again, he grazes my shoulder. It's the first time that our skin has made contact since the day we kissed in my office. Instead of moving away, I let my arm rest gently against Jack's.

Timmy is still speaking—"I know what the critics will say"—but it doesn't hold my attention. Jack catches my eye and bites his lip; I raise a brow back. At that, he rubs his thumb covertly across the top of my wrist, before clasping his hands behind his back.

Not wanting to be outdone, I raise my hand to adjust the strap of my dress but detour at the back of Jack's neck, fingertips tracing from his hairline to his collar.

He lets out an audible sigh. A few heads turn.

My eyes widen. I cough loudly and dramatically to cover up the sound. I gesture to my drink and feign a motion to suggest tequila made its way down my windpipe. Jack shakes with silent laughter beside me.

"Now, I wanted you all to have something as a token of my appreciation," Timmy continues, and I force my focus back toward him. "So with some help from the art department—and from our line producers—we found a little room in the budget for these." Then he holds up one of the sweatshirts we had made: "*The Just OK Gatsby*" written out across the front.

"Let the record reflect that nothing about this was 'just OK' for me," Jack says into my hair.

We slip out of a black car in front of a white two-story split-level, the last property on a dead-end lane. Jack's fingers find my lower back, and my breathing steadies. I realize I don't know how to navigate what's to come and that I've gotten a little in my own head about it on the ride over.

His hand moves to find my own, and he intertwines our fingers as he leads me toward the entrance. He doesn't break his grasp as he unlocks the door or flips the lights or tosses his keys onto the marble island dividing the kitchen and living room. I take in an oak and oxidized steel coffee table I recognize as Arhaus and a sprawling gray-blue sectional.

"Can I get you anything?" he asks, bringing my hand to his mouth and brushing his lips along my knuckles.

"Some water would be great."

As Jack fills two glasses, I take a closer look at the framed pictures lining the bookshelves. A photo of the actor Brent Chase, known mostly for his work top-lining network procedurals, at a party. Another of Brent Chase and his wife, Maria Alvarez, a character actor, at the beach. Brent, Maria, and a few friends in Park City, decked out in bright ski suits.

Jack hands me my drink. I relish the grounding weight of having something to hold. "Did you kill Brent Chase?"

He laughs. "When I needed a place to stay, my agent's assistant found out from his assistant that he'd be filming his show in New York for a while, so this place was available to rent. I didn't want a hotel this time."

"He has great taste." *Stop being nervous. You've already had sex with this man.*

Jack cocks his head. He takes my hand again and holds it tighter this time, a reassurance, and leads me up the floating staircase.

When we enter the bedroom, it's like something clicks into place, and my hesitation evaporates. I want Jack. I have wanted Jack for months. I have wanted Jack for *years*. Now, there's nothing standing in the way of me having him. At least for the night.

Jack turns toward me, his back to the giant bed with its hotel-white sheets and comforter. He gently brushes a hair out of my eyes as he takes the glass out of my hands and sets it down on the empty nightstand. I shove his shoulders gently, and he falls to a seat, his eyes still locked on mine. I stand between his legs, and his hands make their way along my calves, behind my knees, and up my thighs. My nipples make their presence known from beneath the sleek mesh bra I'd purchased for the occasion, and he leans forward and covers them with his mouth, one then the other, leaving two faint wet spots and an aching want. My jaw goes slack.

"I'm going to make this last as long as I possibly can," he says in a voice I can barely hear.

Then his hands find the zipper that runs up the left side of my dress, and he yanks it down and pushes it off my shoulders, watching it fall to the floor. He gazes up at me and runs his hands over my breasts, my stomach, my hips. I let him stare and let myself be on display. I am desperate for him to move his hand between my legs, and instead of waiting, I guide it there, needing to ease the pain.

"*Fuck*, CJ," he moans. "Have you been walking around our set soaking wet like this the whole time?" Before I can answer, he leans in to drag his tongue over my clit and plunges two fingers inside of me. I cry out, a whimpering sound I've never heard myself make before, and arch into the pressure of Jack's touch, urging him deeper.

When I can't take it a second longer, I push him back against the mattress, tugging the polo over his torso and dragging my nails down his ribs as I do.

He smirks at me. "This is not slow."

"We'll do slow later," I say as I crush my lips against his, and I can feel him smile in response. I unbutton his pants and tug them out from under him.

"Condom's in the pocket, if you're in such a hurry."

"Says the man who brought the condom to the party. Did you think we were going to fuck at the bar?"

"It wouldn't be the first time."

I climb onto his lap and feel the press of him through my matching mesh underwear. As I start to rock on top of him, he grips my thighs as if to steady me, but I only roll my hips with more fervor in response.

"Cara," he pants, calling back to the last time we were naked with each other. "I don't even have my knickers off."

"Knickers." I grin and tug at his waistband.

"Please know I wouldn't normally use the word, but I'm willing to role-play a caricature of myself to humor you."

I pull his gray underwear off and let myself take him in as I fish for the condom in his pants pocket. I survey the lines of his body that I'd been surreptitiously reacquainting myself with during filming. The curve of his bicep. The ridge of his collarbone. The divot I remembered at the side of his ass. Now that he's sprawled out in front of me, I can admit to myself that I've been undressing him with my eyes over these weeks.

I rip open the foil packet and slide on the condom, the need to have him inside me urgent now. I move my underwear to the side as I settle back on top of him, a high-pitched moan escaping my lips as I do.

"Cara," he gasps in response, gripping my hip. *Cah-ra.* I could come from the sound of my name on his lips. "You feel fucking incredible, Cara."

I draw him into me fully, throwing back my head as if

to make room, before pressing the heels of my hands into his upper arms and my teeth into his shoulder as I move my hips. His hand grabs my ass as I move my mouth to his ear, snagging his lobe between my teeth and whispering "Yes, I was." He turns to look at me quizzically.

"You were what?"

"Yes, I was soaking wet for you at work."

I watch his pupils darken in response, and he wordlessly grabs my shoulders and flips me over onto my back. His thrusts quicken, and I focus on the movement of our bodies and the glide of his dick inside of me. The heat rising off of us. The faint scent of fancy laundry detergent on the bedding. When my attention lands on Jack's Cupid's bow, the affection I feel for him almost overwhelms me. *How does this end?*

His thumb moves to my clit, and I can't consider anything but the pleasure of being with him in this way. Of this being worth the wait. I press the pads of my fingers into his triceps as I squeeze myself around him and climax, my entire body pulsing. His hand finds the nape of my neck and presses my face to his as he follows, gasping out my name again—*Cah-ra, Cah-ra, Cah-ra.*

He stills and settles his head into the crook of my neck. I lie underneath him, his dick still inside me, and listen to our breathing, savoring the hush as we reorient ourselves in reality.

Jack is the first to stir, raising up to look at me and tracing my cheekbone with his finger. "Let's not wait another five years to do that," he says, kissing the corner of my mouth.

I laugh. "Five minutes?"

"I might need twenty," he jokes.

I roll off of him so that we're opposite each other in bed, facing each other.

My body feels boneless, but my brain is still humming from all the stimuli of the evening: Jack at the party, Jack here, Jack inside me. A man who could probably make me come with one hand tied behind his back. Or both. I need to slow down the thoughts before they spin out of control, so I speak again.

"You really didn't mind leaving early tonight?" I ask.

"Oh, God," he says trailing a finger down my side. My skin feels cool against Brent Chase's Egyptian cotton sheets. "You know, all of those parties were fun the first few years, exciting, but now . . . I don't really have it in me, to be honest. Sometimes I think that if I were a better actor, I wouldn't need to do any of it."

"I—" I only know my brow has crinkled when he reaches up to smooth it. "I felt a little bad dragging you away from it. Because you're the star, and because it is sort of your job—regardless of how good of an actor you are."

Jack shifts so we can make eye contact. "Can I ask you a question?"

"I don't think it's been twenty minutes yet," I tease.

"Do *you* like those parties?"

I smile. "It's not that I dislike them. Just that I'd rather be on set. Or playing with Agnes, or watching movies with Stuart, or . . . lying here. In this bed. With you." I can't quite look at him as I say that last part. But he tips my chin up to demand that I do.

"I'd rather be here than most places."

Then he kisses me, hard. It's the kind of kiss that some-how suggests a different sort of closeness than the sex we just had. I nestle my head into his chest and consider the cocoon he and I have created for ourselves, and I wonder how long it can last.

XVI

Jack

The morning starts the way only one morning ever has before: with CJ in bed next to me.

Her eyes are closed, her arm is tucked under her pillow, and her hair is splayed out everywhere like an abstract painting. I'm too energized to fall back to sleep. I've been staring at the ceiling, motionless, watching as sunlight starts to stream into the room.

I feel CJ begin to stir.

"What time is it?" Her mouth stretches to say each word as she wakes up.

"Just after 6."

She shifts to face me, and I kiss her temple, feeling the warmth of her against my mouth. She snakes her hand down my bare stomach, and I slip my hand under the covers to cup her butt.

"Waking up early means more time together before I have to leave," she mumbles sleepily. "I hate that I have to go."

I hate it too. But that she has other places to be and other people who need her is also a turn-on.

"Agnes is lucky," I say, wondering what Agnes is like and what they're like together as I reach for a section of CJ's hair and twirl it around my finger.

"And I'm lucky," she says, burrowing deeper into her pillow.

"Can I ask you a question?"

"You don't have to ask permission for that."

"You know, you're such a careful and deliberate person . . . but isn't deciding to have a kid a giant risk? Isn't becoming a parent—a single parent—the ultimate relinquishing of control?"

CJ looks away, and I brace for her response.

"I guess . . . there is security and certainty in knowing she will always come first. That her school plays will matter more than a huge movie job. Also, doing it mostly on my own is, I guess, a way of retaining some small amount of control, or at least the illusion of it. I trust and know myself. It's a lot of work this way, but it comes with fewer compromises, less shared decision-making."

She drapes her leg over my hip, and I pull her closer and kiss her lazily, like relaxing into a warm bath after a long day.

"School plays, huh? Will Agnes act? Did you ever?"

"She's dramatic, that's for sure. But me? Please. Stage crew for life." CJ pokes my chest for emphasis. "Stage manager for all four years of high school."

"I would expect nothing less."

"And you? Were you in your school plays?"

I run my hand through my hair, as if to tousle it into place. "It was my punishment. That's how I got into this racket. I was kind of a troublemaker. Always mouthing off in class. And there were never enough boys signing up. So the nuns decided I would do that instead of cleaning chalkboards. I ended up loving it, so maybe the nuns knew something I didn't."

"Don't they always," CJ says drily.

"I think the reason I was acting out was because it seemed like every other kid had something they were passionate about or good at, and I didn't have that yet. Once I found theater, film came right after. I was smitten. I went from the class joker to a movie nerd overnight."

"My favorite kind of nerd." CJ kisses my neck and closes her eyes.

I clear my throat and do my best to maintain a casual tone. "What are you and Agnes getting up to these next few weeks?" I draw circles on her lower back while I can still reach out and touch her. I don't know when she has to leave, and I can't bring myself to ask.

"Lots of playground time. The zoo and the aquarium. She *loves* the La Brea Tar Pits."

"That sounds lovely."

"We've sort of settled into this routine." CJ's eyes are still closed. "I work in really intense bursts, and then we get these wonderful long swaths of time together. But she changes so much so fast. There are days when I come home and she's already asleep in bed, and I feel like I'm seeing an older kid than the one I'd left in the morning. Like she grows when I'm not looking. I hate missing any of it. But I also love the work. And I know it makes me who I am as much as being her mom does."

"Do you have your next project lined up?"

"A few commercials. And a music video. Music videos were my first-ever official credits back in college. I don't want to commit to another movie anytime soon unless it's something big-budget again like *Gatsby* or I love the director's vision. Ideally both."

I nod, like I understand, though that hasn't been my own approach to work at all.

"What about you?" A look of trepidation flashes across CJ's face, one that I haven't seen before.

I realize that I'd been so enmeshed in *Gatsby* and getting to the finish line of this shoot, having a good night's sleep, going on a date with CJ, and shagging her too, that I hadn't thought about exactly what comes after. My brain stretches to think.

"I have this Blumhouse popcorn thriller, *Push It to the Limit*, with Lily Collins. She's the final girl, and I'm her boyfriend, so you know what that means."

"That you're the killer?"

"No, it means I die *second* to last."

CJ laughs. "And is this a passion project?"

"Hardly," I say before I think. It occurs to me that I can't remember the last time I've been particularly passionate about a project or a person, before now. "There's no rest for the weary, as they say. Or did my agent make that up?"

"Ahh," CJ says, shifting to her elbows and taking a good, long look at me before sitting up. "The weary are the ones who need the rest most of all."

"Do you have to? Go?"

"I have to at least get out of this bed to make it a little easier to go." She slips into last night's dress, and I put on the T-shirt of mine she slept in, still smelling of her. We meander downstairs, and I set about brewing a pot of English breakfast.

"So, for our proper date," I say, turning over my shoulder to address CJ, who is perched on a stool at the kitchen island.

CJ picks up her phone. "Next Thursday? When I'm not on a project, that's the night that Stuart comes by for Movie Club with Agnes."

"Movie Club?"

"It's very sophisticated. Absolutely no Disney princesses."

I consult my phone as well. "I'm supposed to go to a Gucci party." I grimace as I scroll through my calendar app. I'm bombarded by blocks of blue for press commitments, patches of purple for parties and events, and, in two weeks, a solid wall of red for *Push It to the Limit*.

"I don't suppose you'd want to come to a Gucci—" I start, but CJ cuts me off.

"Not exactly my scene. And awfully . . . public."

"Right." I flip through, trying to find a worthy window of time.

"What about next weekend? Agnes is going to be with her father, actually. He's back in town for a little while."

"There is . . . so . . ." I stammer, at a loss. "I have these press engagements for the Bone Collector series. There's a new Marvel premiere. A Men in Hollywood luncheon. I can get out of some of this—I just have to check." I squint at my calendar again. *When am I going to sleep? Or read the stacks of scripts Delia sent me?* "On Tuesday, I'm going on *Hot Ones*, but breakfast before?" I cringe at myself for even suggesting it. *How is there no time in my schedule for the one thing I actually want to do?*

CJ shakes her head. "For the next two weeks, before she starts camp, my days are for Agnes. Plus, you really should do *Hot Ones* on an empty stomach."

"You know about *Hot Ones*?"

"Jack, I like old movies, but I live on Planet Earth."

"Two weeks is when *Push It to the Limit* starts." The kettle screeches behind me. I wince at it and myself. As I pour the water over the Fortnum and Mason tea bags, my gaze drifts to CJ, and I wonder when we'll have our next opportunity for a morning like this. *My God. Pathetic. I can fix this.* "I'll go to the Gucci thing early. Or skip it. I'll figure it out." I push out of my mind the conversation I'll surely have to have with Delia about playing nice with brands for red-carpet priority and future ad campaigns.

CJ smiles, but it's strained. "Next Thursday it is."

I fetch a carton of milk from the otherwise empty refrigerator. "It's not a proper cuppa without it," I tell her, distributing a splash into each of our mugs and trying to shift the mood back to our morning-after haze.

But the bubble has burst. I watch as CJ's eyes trace over my face, then down my forearms, before landing on the counter.

"I should probably get going," she sighs, resigned.

I want to wipe the smudge of last night's eyeliner from her face, but suddenly that gesture feels too intimate. My chest clenches. I've fucked this up before we even got started.

An hour later, I'm horizontal on Brent's gigantic couch, wallowing. The birds are chirping so loudly outside that they nearly drown out Monica, Chandler, Joey, Rachel, Phoebe, and Ross on Brent's also enormous television screen. This is my comfort watch; these are the friends I spend time with when I can't be with my own.

I hold my phone above me as I scan everything stuffed into my calendar. Any plans I had to see Tom and his family, watch movies, boil a pot of pasta for myself, are all out the window. I'm not ready to be on set again. I don't want to play with puppies for a digital magazine feature in hopes of manufacturing a viral moment. After the next project, I'm signed for a Reese Witherspoon movie about a mother finding herself against the backdrop of the women's liberation movement. It looks like I'm set to play her son. *That can't be right. Can it?*

Nick in Gatsby is the closest I've come to a real starring role in a movie with major studio backing. I know I have to leverage this moment. *It's hard to get on the carousel once you hop off,* Delia once told me. Does that apply if the carousel is a movie about an AI ghost?

My phone buzzes. Tom.

"He's free at last! How was the party last night?" his text reads, followed by a picture of his three-year-old daughter Sabrina with a colander over her head. "We got absolutely wild over here."

I haven't seen him since I got to town, but he under-stands what this life is like. In some ways, he's jealous of all I'm juggling, and he's said as much. But he has both a career as a working actor *and* the normalcy. He has an actual life—*the* actual life—that I professed to want over drinks with CJ at the fake Bemelmans: from bachelor party to wedding to streaming-series regular to house to baby. I try to will myself to text him back, but I can't reckon with the feelings it surfaces, and instead, I turn my attention back to the show, watching Ross summon the courage to drink a glass of fat in order to convince Rachel to join him at his big science party.

That's it, I think. I know what I need to do.

XVII

CJ

As the princess waits to be rescued from a dragon, she races through the hallway of our home screaming "You'll never get me!!!" The dragon roars and wonders at what point she can explain to the princess that it's on her to save herself.

Staying in character as the dragon is an uphill battle today. As Agnes bolts away from me, my thoughts drift back to Jack and our conversation around Brent Chase's kitchen island. *I have a date with Jack Felgate!* I really try to sell it to myself. Which makes me feel like I'm starring in my own adaptation of *Bye Bye Birdie*, where I've won the chance to spend time with the Swoony Celebrity and not an actual man I have actual feelings for.

It's one date, crammed into a sea full of other commitments, for both of us, and the logistical reality of it turning into something more feels . . . impossible. After Thursday, I'll be here, and he'll be back on set, sucked into another world, another summer camp experience. I can't picture how we even communicate meaningfully across the chasm. Something I immediately liked about Jack, even when we first met at that bar, is that he focuses on what's in front of him. He takes his work seriously but not himself, a rare combination for someone in front of the camera. His eyes lock on whoever he's speaking with, never scanning past for someone more important. If I'm not in front of Jack, I'm not sure how to hold his attention.

We only guaranteed each other one date, but I've gotten ahead of myself, already imagining the corners of LA that I'll show him or what it would be like to watch a movie while *physically* together. I need to level with myself: Our one-night stand from five years ago won't have a second chapter, so much as a brief epilogue.

My heart feels leaden in my chest. Coming down from the adrenaline of weeks of shooting capped by last night is its own kind of hangover. I try to focus on where I am *right now*, in my perfect little bungalow, in my favorite pair of cutoffs and my timeworn LA Dodgers T-shirt, but images of Jack and I flash into my head, like my brain is flipping channels against my will.

There is a part of me that wants to text my high-school friends group chat—the one that occasionally lives vicariously through me, as its last remaining single member—to dish about my steamy night and try to bring back the frothy high of being with him. But there would be two warring factions: one side that would say, "A movie star?! This is the most exciting thing to happen to us in years!" and the other that would question, just as I had, "What are you doing getting involved with a famous actor? It's so unlike you."

But the version of events that would come through over text would be an oversimplification, and my disappointment with the incompatibility of our lives is just as much about me as him. *I like my life. I chose it.* And it's not as if Jack didn't choose his. It isn't my place to tell him, "You're working too hard, you shouldn't say yes to everything, you're overexposing yourself." I'm not his agent, manager, or life coach. These are realizations he has to come to himself. "A man," my mother used to say, "can only meet you where he is. You can't go on a date with Stef from *Pretty in Pink* and expect him to be Blaine."

"*Mommy!* You were supposed to catch me!"

Agnes is back, and she's right. I crouch down to grab her, flipping her upside down. "Give me your jewels!" I roar, and she squeals. *How much longer will I have this?* If I can take any page from Jack's book, it's to be present, to treasure the beautiful uncertainty of parenting while it's right in front of me.

The doorbell rings—the burgers, fries, and extravagantly melty milkshakes I ordered have arrived.

"Hey, sweetie, why don't you get changed so you don't get ketchup on your princess dress?" I say, twirling Agnes toward her room.

I open the door to a young guy with a fuzzy mustache holding a big brown paper bag filled with our food. And, just behind him, Jack.

"What are you doing here?"

"This is 2078 Norwalk Avenue?"

"Sorry, yes." I look past him toward Jack. "I was talking to him."

Mustache boy twists to look over his shoulder and then spins his entire body to face Jack. "Oh shit, you're that guy from *Flames Flicker Eternal*. Can I get a picture? My girlfriend *loves* you."

Jack searches my face for approval. I shrug. "Just don't get my house in the background."

Jack smiles good-naturedly as they snap a selfie. The only evidence of his discomfort is in his eyes. The guy is already sharing the photo as he walks back to his car, if his urgent thumbing at his phone is any indication.

"How do you know where I live?" I ask Jack, as if that's what matters.

"I told Manny I needed it to send a thank-you gift." He waves this detail away like it's a gnat.

Then, he looks at me, eyes shining with sincerity, and says, "I'm drinking the fat."

"Is that a Britishism?"

"Do you know the television show *Friends*?"

"*Jack*."

"Right, sorry," he says quickly, propping his hand on the doorframe as if to steady himself. "Do you know the episode where Ross drinks the fat? To convince Rachel to go to the dorky science party with him?"

"I guess . . ." I shift the bag of food in my arms. *What are we doing here?*

"Well, I realized this morning, that's what *I* need to do. I need to drink the fat. I need to do the thing I'm afraid of. Well, Ross doesn't ultimately drink the fat, but he was willing to, and I think that's the mindset I need to be in."

"So . . . drinking the fat is a metaphor?"

"I'm going to take six months away from acting. From my press commitments. All of it. I told Delia I'm off everything until it's time to promote *Gatsby*. I've been saying yes to anything and everything, and I don't know how I can't expect other people to take me seriously if I don't start to take myself a little more seriously."

"So no acting? Really?"

"Not unless Cecily Close comes calling."

This earns him a laugh. The odds of the notoriously reclusive director taking on a new project, let alone calling up Jack for it, are about as high as Peter Bogdanovich directing another movie from beyond the grave.

"Can you afford to do that? Financially?"

"I'm fine. I have money saved," Jack says, running a hand through his hair. "Saying yes to everything has been good for my bank account."

I set the delivery order down. "Jack, if you're doing this for me . . ." I start.

"No," he says firmly. "This is for me. I know why I got into acting, and it wasn't to be the British ambassador for Nespresso." He pauses. "But one of the things I'd like to do with my newfound time is spend it with you. And go on real dates, but also just—and tell me if I'm being presumptuous here—be with you. On a couch, in a bed, those sorts of places."

Hookups on a bar be damned: This is the sexiest Jack has ever been to me.

"But I should tell you—" His face grows more serious, and my smile sags.

"I am still going on *Hot Ones*."

I laugh, and like it's a full-body release. "Oh yeah, of course. You gotta go on *Hot Ones*. It would be career suicide to pass that up."

XVIII

Jack

"Are you ready?"

CJ sits across from me at a metal table, not unlike the ones we shared on the lot. She stares at me intently.

"I'm ready," I tell her. Her hair is down, a way she never wears it while she's working, and I'm smitten with how perfectly it frames her face.

"Are you sure?" she presses. "Because what you are about to eat is going to change your life. There will be a before, and there will be an after."

"I'm ready! Anticipation has built." I am carefully cradling a heavy taco al pastor. CJ has her own trio in front of her, but she's too focused on my meal to look at her own. She leans forward as I take my first bite.

The combination of flavors—char, salt, tang, sweetness, spice—hits me hard. I cover my mouth. "OK, wow."

We're at an unassuming spot in Atwater Village, the first stop on CJ's "LA on the other side of the velvet rope" tour. "You sound like a food blogger," I teased when she shared her plan, masking my genuine gratitude that

119

she knows of actual places where we won't get papped—the mythical establishments I swore existed when pitching her on a date. Up until now, my version of LA has been the "Hey, look this way!" version of LA.

In my excitement over my second bite, I unleash sauce onto my linen shirt.

"Wait, wait, I got it." CJ digs through her purse and triumphantly pulls out a Tide pen. As she wields it standing over me, I put my hands on her hips and pull her closer.

"I wish I could say that I have this because I'm a mom, but you should know this is just who I am. A person who has carried on-the-go stain remover since college." She laughs at herself and taps the wet patch on my chest, letting her finger linger before breaking our contact and sitting back down to her meal.

"Actually, I knew that about you even if I didn't know *that* about you." I watch CJ tuck into her first taco with scholarly fascination. "When's the last time you were here?"

"Agnes and I came right before *Gatsby*. I try to check off my favorites ahead of a big project, knowing I won't get my fix for a while. Agnes only eats the chips, but someday."

"That's what I've missed most about all the coming and going the last few years. I've barely been able to visit any of my favorite pubs in London. Or, frankly, have an actual meal. Most of what I eat is crafty on set or those tiny little appetizers at parties," I say, going in for another bite of taco.

"Why not between projects?"

"I have small pockets, mostly reserved for hanging out in my flat in my underwear. And seeing my family," I tack on.

"They're all in London, your family?"

I nod. "Yep, Mum, Dad, and my older brother, Mark."

"Older brother! How am I only hearing about this now?"

"He's three years older." I pause, trying to find the best way to describe Mark. "He's a really nice chap."

CJ drops her chin. "That's the kind of thing you say about, like, your friend's husband you met one time."

"Well, he is!" I insist with a laugh. *Will she think I'm a monster for not being best mates with my own brother?* "So," I say, reaching for the napkin dispenser. "We were never really close growing up. Now, he's a banker. Married to a lovely woman he met at uni. Lives down the road from my parents. We just . . . don't have much in common. I think the only thing we've texted about in the last five years is Arsenal."

"Really?"

I nod, fishing my phone out of my trouser pocket. I scroll up through our most recent exchanges: articles about our favorite player's injury, forecasts about how the team may perform that season, celebratory emojis when they did well, curse words when they did not. I hand my phone to her.

"There are a lot of 'bollocks' here," CJ notes.

"They haven't played well in a long time."

"If anything ever happened, he'd be there in a heartbeat," I add as I tuck my phone away, acknowledging Mark's goodness, if not our closeness. "My family." I never quite know how to put this. "They're kind people. They just don't really feel like mine, if that makes any sense."

CJ's eyes go a little sad. "How do they feel about . . ." She swirls her hand about indicating my general form.

"Me being out with you? I haven't told them." She rolls her eyes. "Me being an actor? I think it confused them for a long time. They assumed I'd grow out of it, and then when I didn't, panic set in. But seeing me perform on the West End, I think they finally got that I was doing this for real."

"Not when you got *Flames Flicker Eternal*?"

"You mean my big full-frontal moment? No, that didn't go far with my parents."

"I just meant it was a big . . . part." She trips over her word choice. "I mean, an *important* part for you."

"No, no, keep talking about how big my parts are. I love it."

CJ giggles and shakes her head and takes a sip of her lemonade. "Too much."

"It didn't seem like too much, the other—"

"Jack. My *God*." She swats at my forearm and lets her hand rest there, a finger tracing from my wrist to my elbow. A moment passes. I don't know how much touching is allowed in public, and I don't want to push it.

CJ picks up a plastic fork and holds it to her mouth, like a microphone. "Now, tell me, Jack, why is it that you decided to bare all on the BBC?" she asks in her best faux-journalist voice.

"Well, I figured, women are expected to do it all the time. Why should it be such a big deal for me?" I tap the fork's prongs with concern. "Is this thing on?"

After lunch, CJ drives us to our second stop. No GPS, twisting and turning as the roads become narrower, ascending through the canyons. Along the way, she points out where various celebrities once lived as we cross Mulholland Drive: Madonna, Warren Beatty, Joni Mitchell, Jack Nicholson.

"We used to cruise up here all the time in high school."

"Did you know anyone who lived over here?"

She whips her head as if I've lobbed a horrific accusation her way. "*Please.* I'm a valley girl," she says, fake tossing her hair. "We mostly liked looking at all the big houses."

"Is that what teens in the valley do for fun?"

"No, but it's what my friends and I did for fun."

"Do your friends work in movies too?"

"Some of them. A lot of their parents worked in the business, which made filmmaking seem like less of an impenetrable fortress. Between them and Stuart, this world seemed almost normal. Which, obviously, it is not. But my closest friends from growing up mostly left and did something else. One's a doctor in Vermont; another's an event planner in the Bay Area. Another just moved to Chicago for a job at the Art Institute. We're in touch, but not as much as I want to be."

I relate to that last part, and there's comfort in knowing my distance from those closest to me—Tom so nearby, George back in England now—might not be the rarity it sometimes feels like it is: a product of my highly specific and sometimes selfish life choices.

"What is this place?" I ask as CJ pulls up to what could only be described as a wooden shack, not unlike the kind of place where we'd buy fresh fish during summer holidays in Brighton.

She arches an eyebrow. "You'll see."

We climb out of the car, and my skin prickles. It's unclear if it's a response to the cool, summer night air, the streaks of pink and purple in the sky, the company, or . . . this evening altogether. I look at CJ looking at the sunset, and I wrap my arms around her from behind, leaning my cheek against the top of her head. I feel myself getting unexpectedly choked up, and I blink, not wanting to get caught in . . . what exactly? Turning emotional over a fully cinematic moment, surrounded by hilltops with this woman I feel like I know better than I possibly can?

CJ tilts her head. "Wait until you try this place's ice cream. It's the perfect soft serve. They've been here *forever*. Jane Fonda used to come here when she was a kid."

She reaches for my hand and tugs me toward the shack.

"We have to eat it in the car, though," she turns back to tell me. "Because there might be mountain lions."

"Right," I say, hoping that I'm successfully downplaying my alarm.

CJ grabs the doorknob, but it doesn't turn. She knocks. No answer. "It's summer hours. They're supposed to be open until 9." She knocks again, calling out, "Hello?" She shakes her head. "They said they'd be open."

"We can go somewhere else."

"But we're supposed to go *here*."

This is not about the ice cream, I'm realizing. It's that CJ had a plan, and CJ doesn't like when her plans change. I pull her to me, and she takes a deep breath in and holds it before letting it out. Then she laughs.

"I'm not sure if you've noticed, but I like when things go a certain way. When the vision in my head comes to life."

"And I'm very attracted to that about you. I've never met someone so capable of knowing what they want and making it happen. You're rather good at being in charge."

She laughs louder. "That's a nice way of saying 'bossy.'"

"Exceedingly competent," I say, and she relaxes into me. To be able to touch her this way, to openly embrace after what felt like an eternity of restraining ourselves, sends reverberations throughout my entire body. I wonder if I'll ever get used to it. Part of me hopes not.

I kiss her forehead, urging her brows to unfurrow. "I have an idea."

She looks at me quizzically.

"Oh, just trust me," I say, amused by her inability to let me take over. "I'll be directing you this time."

Her mouth opens to argue, but I just grab her hand.

Twenty-five minutes later, we're standing outside the Burbank Costco, each of us with a cone in our hands. Chocolate for her, swirl for me.

"You're right," she says, her tongue gliding up her ice cream in a way I don't think she realizes is seductive. "It's maybe the second-best soft serve I've ever had. How did you know to come here? To this very American institution?"

"Sabrina's daughter, Tom, is absolutely crazy for it. She's always begging to go to Costco."

"Tom's your friend who had the bachelor party?"

"*Stag* party," I tease. "But yes, we've been friends since uni, and he's my person—the one I go to for everything."

At this, her face transitions to a distant stare. "That used to be my mom, for me."

I can feel my heart expand in my chest, and I reach for her hand.

CJ sighs and nods. "It always felt like the two of us against the world. I mean, financially, I think Stuart helped some when I was growing up, but she never wanted to rely on anyone else. But she had to work *a lot*. And that's why I try to be careful about my hours. When Agnes is older, I want her to feel proud of the work I do but not like it's *all* I do."

I nod, picturing teenage CJ doing her homework by herself at the kitchen table.

"It sometimes feels like an impossible balance to strike. Which is maybe where my obsession with planning comes in," she says, returning to her ice cream.

We stand in the twilight at the edge of a vast California parking lot, and I think about the last decade of my life and all the things I could have never planned. "But some accidents are happy."

"Agnes." She smiles.

"Our meeting at a random bar—and then meeting again years later," I add.

She blushes. "Ending a first date at the Burbank Costco."

Single best date of my life, I can't bring myself to say aloud.

XIX

CJ

"You have a decision to make," I tell Jack with the utmost seriousness. "Choose wisely."

He sits up straighter, playing along.

I slouch cross-legged, facing him on Brent Chase's couch. Jack bites the inside of his cheek, and after two months of dating, I know this is what he does when he's thinking.

"*Romancing the Stone*," Jack says with a nod, like he's answering a Double Jeopardy question.

"That was going to be my pick for next week!"

"And look who beat you to it."

For the last eight Thursdays, we've had a standing date while Stuart and Agnes have Movie Club back at my house. Sometimes, I go over to Jack's, and we order in and take turns choosing a movie. Sometimes, we go out to under-the-radar restaurants or repertory screenings, and Jack brings along a baseball cap and sunglasses just in case. When we're in public, eyes linger on him, and the Twitter account Jack Felgate Out of Context has posted a few blurry phone snaps of our excursions, but nothing has hit mass media.

And though we've spent plenty of time in Jack's bed, I always end up back in my own. I pull myself out of Jack's arms before sleep hits so I can be there when Agnes wakes up. I haven't introduced Jack to her or Stuart yet, so my place has been off-limits for him.

When Jack showed up at my door, I wasn't sure I really believed he would take the time off that he promised. I trusted that he intended to but felt less confident that he'd be able to see it through. What if he realized he actually missed the parties? What if my life was just too boring—not for me, but for someone accustomed to a series of highly produced outings, one after the next?

Then, weeks became months, and Jack became more . . . content. He's lighter on his feet. Like someone has taken a coat hanger out from between his shoulder blades. And for the first time in as long as I can remember, I allow blocks of time to go unaccounted for, enjoying each moment with Jack instead of jumping ahead to what the next one will be.

Jack queues up the movie, and I get up to grab the popcorn he popped from the counter. "Stovetop? I'm impressed."

"What can I say? There's also a bottle of that rosé we had at the Italian place last week."

I pull the wine out of the fridge. "You picked this up?"

"Between my very busy schedule of not working and

also not working, yes, I managed to get a bottle of wine." I look across the room at him, lounging in sweatpants that hang low from his hips, and bite my lower lip as I register the way my body responds to the sight of him.

"Well, it's not like you're not doing *anything*," I counter as I sit back down next to him.

"Yes, I am very busy," he says, kissing my forehead and wrapping an arm around my neck. "Had my online UCLA screenwriting class, and then"—another kiss on my neck now—"thought about this. And then I went for a hike." His teeth catch the flesh of my earlobe, and I reach under the hem of his T-shirt. "Then I thought about this some more."

"Very busy." I swing my legs over his lap as he hits play, and he pulls the clip from my hair and runs his fingers along my scalp.

"See," Jack says about thirty minutes into the movie. "This is exactly it. Making movies with your friends, like Michael Douglas and Danny DeVito did." He's brimming with nostalgia for something he's never experienced.

I scan his face and grab the remote to hit pause. "What's your dream project?"

"Something like this, to be honest. Something that blends genres, that feels like it's for adults."

"So, no superheroes, then?"

He scoffs. "Only if their superpowers are that they can banter like Harry and Sally."

"Or howl like Nicholas Cage in *Moonstruck*?"

"Except in our movie, when he does, he breaks the sound barrier."

"Our movie?" I ask. "You'll have to take that up with my agent."

"I'll act. You'll direct. We'll both produce."

"Direct?"

"Oh, come on. Who has more vision and ideas than you? Loads of production designers become directors."

I've only ever given half a thought to directing while on set, seeing a shot being framed in a way I didn't think served the story best, watching rush jobs that didn't allow gaffers time to light the actors properly, or witnessing an entire department underserved due to bad budgeting. But I've never brought the idea home with me. Between making my way in production design and raising Agnes, taking on anything more always feels like too much. It's fun to joke around like this, but the idea of working with Jack again makes anxiety bubble up in my stomach. The same fears that plagued me on *Gatsby* bounce around in my head: *How would we handle being in a relationship in front of an entire cast and crew? Would anyone be able to take me seriously?*

I let the comment lie. "Well, it looks like you found your passion project."

"This right here is my passion project." He squeezes my thigh, and my cheeks warm.

"What about you?" He seems nervous for my answer.

"I don't know if you mean work or us," I reply, considering what to say next. "But *this*—us—it's so much more right and real than I could've hoped."

"Because I'm a fake celebrity type?"

"Because I've never had this before. You know, life

hardly ever feels like the movies, which has been a great disappointment as a cinephile." I laugh. "My other relationships have been . . . pleasantly convenient. Or with guys who seem like they'd be right for me but turn out not to be. But us, and this . . . meeting you when I least expected it, *twice* . . . that's cinematic."

"And you don't even have to build a bar," he says.

"And you don't have to do costume fittings."

"*I* get to be your set piece." He beams and kisses my temple, and when my phone dings from the coffee table, he passes it to me. A photo from Stuart of Agnes curled up asleep on the couch. When I turn my screen to show it to Jack, he gives me a restrained smile.

"What?" I ask.

"When are you going to let me meet them?"

"I don't know," I tell him, honestly. I look down at my hands, interlaced between my legs, Michael Douglas and Kathleen Turner so long forgotten that a screensaver has taken their place.

"I don't want to pressure you. I really don't. I know that this is a very big thing, for Agnes to know me. But it also feels like . . . well, they're over there, and I'm over here, and you and I can't be together until we're all together. They're this giant piece of who you are. And I want—I need—to know all of you."

"We're very together." I shake my head. "But you're . . . not wrong. And I want you to meet them, to know that part of me. It's just . . ."

"What can I do?" Jack asks with raw vulnerability.

"You're doing everything." I run my finger along his lips. I can't explain it to him because I can't quite admit it to myself: that bringing Jack home, for me, feels permanent.

I hit play on the movie and move my head to his lap.

XX

CJ

When I tell Stuart about my resistance to Jack coming over, he scoffs at me.

"You have a handsome, kind, movie-star boyfriend who adores you," he says, voice oozing sarcasm. "Why would you want to let him meet your friends and family?"

I give him my angstiest scowl, and he softens. "Listen, honey, you do a wonderful job protecting Agnes; you really do. But Jack is an important person in your life at this point, and he can't know you without knowing her and—if I can be so bold—knowing *me*. I'm not suggesting you tell her that you're fucking him—"

"*Stuart.*"

"But having a 'friend' for dinner . . . surely this is something we all can handle."

It's hard to make a case against this, so I give up trying. I invite Jack over for Chinese food and Movie Club the following Thursday. The entire week leading up to it, I walk around feeling like I've left the oven on or all my kitchen cabinet doors open.

I'm setting the table for the third time in twenty minutes when Jack rings the doorbell. He smiles boyishly as I let him in, a bottle of red wine in his hands.

"Sorry I'm a few minutes late. The Lyft driver got turned around," Jack says quickly, nervously. It puts me at ease knowing it's not just me who's been reeling.

He crosses through the threshold, and we try to hug casually, but I feel the press of his nose into my hair. I watch his eyes take in Agnes, hiding behind my legs, then Stuart, then the details of my house: the framed vintage posters of *Cabaret* and *Paper Moon* on the buttermilk walls; the blown-up black-and-white photograph of my mother, taken by Stuart the year before I was born; the dark-green velvet couch, a reupholstered Rose Bowl flea find. I'm relieved that despite the presence of a four-year-old, my house is as neat as my office is messy.

"Wow, this home," Jack says, and it's like I exhale for the first time all day. "I'm Jack," he says, extending his hand to Stuart.

The hand goes ignored in favor of an embrace. "Please," Stuart says. "And thank you, CJ, for passing along my wine preferences and, Jack, for obliging. The record has been updated to reflect your ass-kissing."

"Permanent record, I hope," Jack says earnestly, and Stuart gives him a full-throated cackle as I beam. But Stuart isn't the difficult customer.

Jack bends down now, addressing Agnes at her level. "Hi, Agnes. I'm Jack. It's nice to meet you."

Agnes doesn't respond, but she doesn't bolt either. For

her, it's a start. When he asked about bringing her a gift, I told him not to, but now that we're here, I'm not sure if I was right.

I clap my hands. "Time for dinner!" *Calm down*, I remind myself.

As I unbox our lo mein and string beans, Jack opens the wine, and Stuart pours water. Agnes hops into her chair, and we all do the same.

"So, Jack, CJ tells me you're from London," Stuart says, reaching for the fried rice. "Well, I should say, first, your Wikipedia page told me that you were from London. But then CJ did too."

"Stuart," I chide. I could've timed how long it would take him to bring up Jack's celebrity to the minute.

"I *am* from London."

"Not one of the posh parts, I hope," Stuart continues.

"No, not one of the posh parts. One of the deeply average parts."

"Now that's what I like to hear. I'm a Leeds man myself."

"He *was* a Leeds man," I clarify. "He hasn't lived there in fifty years." I glance over at Agnes, who is more focused on her sesame chicken than Jack's presence.

"Left when I was eighteen and never looked back."

"That accent?" I drop my voice to a whisper. "Basically fake."

"You take that back!" Stuart says with Shakespearean flair.

Jack laughs. Then I laugh. Then Stuart laughs. My whole body relaxes all at once.

"Don't worry," Jack says. "I already knew that too. Because I also read *your* Wikipedia page."

"Is that right?" Stuart asks, intrigued and charmed.

"It is. I'm a big fan. You should have seen me carry on about *Wheels of Steel* when CJ told me *her* Stuart was Stuart Blitz."

I had kept Stuart in the dark about Jack's love of his movies, wanting Jack to have the opportunity to tell him himself.

Stuart winks at me. "He's a keeper."

Jack and I lock eyes and smile, and Stuart refills our wineglasses. "OK, Jack, what other movies do you love?"

Jack casts a look at Agnes, who is making her way through a mound of white rice. "Well, *Fantasia* is one of my all-time favorites."

Agnes looks up, and her eyes go wide. "Mine too," she says quietly.

"Yours too?!" Jack says, incredulous. "Maybe we could watch that tonight?"

"Can we, Mommy? *Please?*" She clasps her hands together in desperation.

"I don't know . . . we just watched it yesterday," I say.

"Come on, I really want to watch it too," Jack chimes in. "And I didn't see it yesterday."

"Oh, *alright.*" I fake relent.

"Yes!!!" Agnes cries out, grinning at Jack, her coconspirator.

"Smooth," I mouth to Jack, knowing he's been cramming for this like a final exam, turning to his friend Tom, who has a three-year-old, for coaching and advice. I'm touched by his effort and also by their friendship.

"Now that that's settled, Jack," Stuart chimes in. "Talk to me about what you love about *Wheels of Steel*."

XXI

Jack

The theme is rainbows, and predictably, CJ has gone all-out. Crystals hang from fishing line strung between trees, catching the sunlight and casting prisms across surfaces. Stuart and I were charged with melting chunks of crayon, pouring them into molds to spell Agnes's name, and packaging them up for party favors. CJ baked and iced cupcakes and set them out on mini painter's palettes, and I filled the divots with sprinkles of all colors and sizes.

I'm in the backyard setting up tables for five-year-old attendees when Agnes emerges, followed by Stuart.

"Oh, good," I say to the birthday girl. "Just the lady I was looking for. Tell me, do these tables look right for you and your friends?"

"Yes, Jackie." She giggles. Agnes had started calling me "Jackie" after five or so visits. "This is big," CJ insisted. "It means she likes you."

Since meeting Stuart and Agnes two months ago, I've upgraded to sleepovers with CJ at her house. I leave in the mornings to get coffee or bagels or just go for a stroll in a town where no one walks, then come back like I haven't been there all night. It's an involved charade that I'm not sure Agnes buys or cares about, but there's almost something comforting about having a mundane routine. I find I like being forced out for fresh air.

Five minutes before the party's official start time, I hear a familiar voice. Tom breezes through the back door. "Sorry we're early. I know it's awfully rude. But Sabrina was in our bed at 6 a.m. asking if we could go to the party yet, and for the first time in LA history, we didn't hit any traffic."

I lean in to hug Tom and his wife, Molly, before crouching down for a high five from Sabrina. "Thanks for being here, you three."

"You kidding? This is what my weekends look like anyway. I'm just thrilled this one's with a best mate instead of a bunch of film-finance bros I'm meant to make conversation with."

"Well, thank you still." I wave as Molly and Sabrina take off to play with the bubbles.

"Is he here yet?" Tom asks.

I scan the scene. Today's the day I meet Garrett, Agnes's dad, and Tom knows I've been wringing my hands about it. I don't feel threatened, exactly. He and CJ were work friends who tried to make it as something more and never could. Not that different from how it had been with Ginny and me, CJ and I realized. But Garrett will always be an ensemble player in their lives, and I need him to respect me, at a minimum.

"I don't see him, but I'm going off the photo in Agnes's room. If he shaved his beard or something—I wouldn't know him."

"What else do we have on him?"

"CJ described him as the strong, silent kind. And said not to bring up the Lakers because once he starts, he can't stop."

"Ahh. A sports guy. So she does not have a type."

I knock his shoulder with mine.

"Driving lesson Tuesday?" he asks, shoving me back.

"That'd be great." When I first arrived in LA for the *Gatsby* shoot, I didn't expect I'd have any downtime, and I wasn't concerned with how I'd get around. The public transit system here isn't as accustomed to a famous face as the Tube is, and by now, the reliance on Ubers and CJ has started to take a toll.

"OK, hold please," Tom says. "I'm being summoned for the change of clothes already."

I turn my attention to CJ, who is milling around in a striped cardigan and her perfectly worn-in jeans, patting people on their arms with a relaxed demeanor that belies the effort I watched her put into this day. Last week, she told me that she had wondered if her life would be boring to me. I actually laughed so hard I had to sit down. "I'm sorry," I said as I caught my breath. "But your life is far more fascinating to me than you could ever realize. And I don't think you know the depths of the monotony I was accustomed to suffering through." Certain Hollywood events really are magical, but they are the exception: The vast majority of those things are held at the same five places with interchangeable guest lists featuring exactly three people with whom I genuinely want to chat—if I'm lucky.

I don't miss most of it, and the feeling is mutual, it seems. At first, my absence from the scene was noted, with the trades reporting breathlessly—and speculating wildly—on my decision to withdraw from the Lily Collins movie. Then, gossip sites began to refer to me as "reclusive," wondering what had happened and suggesting perhaps it had to do with an apparent split from my "longtime love" Ginny Friedrich, though no one could say for sure. But when there was little left to say, the public was quick to move on, anointing another younger Brit named Barnaby Cross as "the internet's new boyfriend," which is just fine with me. The only boyfriend I want to be is CJ's.

"Daddy!" I hear Agnes yelp, running toward Garrett, who I see closing the sliding door with one hand and carrying a stack of pizzas with the other.

"Happy birthday, sweetheart!" He sets the boxes down and scoops her up. I am surprised at how envious I feel of him. Agnes likes me, but I will never be this. It's a little painful to witness.

He is about a head taller than me, with broad shoulders and a healthy beard. He looks like the type who might have played, if not American football at university, then baseball, at the very least.

I watch CJ greet him, kissing him lightly on the cheek and leading him my way.

"Garrett, this is my boyfriend, Jack."

"Glad to meet you," Garrett says, offering a firm handshake.

"Same," I say. I'm not sure how to read him. *What's a natural dynamic for the two of us, and can I call up any examples that aren't from movies?*

"I should go finish putting out the party favors." CJ pats my arm.

"Already done," I say.

"Amazing. Then I'm going to grab the cash for the face painter."

"I took care of that."

"You didn't pay for her, did you?"

"Of course not, because I knew how cross you would be if I did."

Four months into our relationship, I am constantly in search of ways to support CJ or make her life easier, but I'm finding it next to impossible.

"Well, thank you." CJ runs a hand down my arm, and I catch myself preening over the physical attention. "OK, plates for pizza."

She heads inside, leaving me alone with Garrett and effectively throwing me to the wolves.

"So, CJ says you were away on a big shoot."

"Yeah, just got back from Prague."

He has a sort of weathered look, one that I understand women find appealing.

"I love Prague," I say reflexively. "Went there on holiday

for the first time when I was eighteen, the summer before my first year at uni. Did a little backpacking trip through eastern Europe. I would love to go back. It's been a long time since I've been." *Why am I saying all of this, and why can't I stop?*

"I didn't get to see much of the city, but it seems nice. Historic."

"And what now?"

"Now?" He repeats my question back to me. "Now, I've got about another two weeks until it's onto the next. You know how it is. No rest for the wicked." His tone is weary yet conspiratorial, and I wonder if it's a good or bad sign I can no longer relate.

"What about you?" He shoves his hands in his pockets.

"Well, I put a pause on projects for now—" I force myself to stand straighter.

"Oh yeah?"

"I'm taking some time off. I was burnt out, needed a break. Hopefully there will be a career for me to go back to when I'm ready." I intend to sound casual, but only after the words are out do I realize I've come off as unsure of myself, like I've accidentally shown CJ's ex a tender bruise.

"I doubt you have anything to worry about."

"Oh yeah, why's that?" I brace for any number of snarky things he could say.

"Because I've seen your work. You're the real deal. There's always room for the real deal."

"That's . . ." I trail off. "Well, I appreciate that." I try not to let my shock at Garrett's casual generosity register externally. Apparently only one of us was viewing this as a pissing match. "Hey, so, uh, say a person is relatively new to LA and wants to get into the Lakers . . ." I start.

XXII

CJ

I'm cutting pizzas into kid-size half slices when I hear the door open. Watching Garrett walk into the room and approach me, it's hard to imagine that there was a time when I felt something more for him.

"Do you need any help?" he asks.

I open my mouth, my stock response already prepared, but Garrett beats me to the punch.

"No, no, I got it," he mimics jovially.

We both laugh as he makes his way over to my side of the kitchen counter.

"This thing with Jack . . . it seems like it's going well."

I stop myself from giving a perfunctory answer—I owe that much to Agnes's dad—and let myself actually contemplate the truth. I would never have imagined that the Jack I met five years ago or the one I re-met on set would be the Jack setting up for Agnes's party today. "It is," I say simply. Garrett knows me well enough to extrapolate.

"It's good you're letting him help out a little bit. Or more than you ever let me."

I nod. Garrett and I both acknowledge that my stubborn independence was one of our relationship's many stumbling blocks.

"Nice," he continues. "*A right proper bloke*," he adds, trying for an accent.

"How many Bond films have you seen, and that's the best you've got?" I tease, grateful to him for being this kind of ex. I don't need Garrett to like Jack—it had barely occurred to me to wonder if he would—but it doesn't hurt.

"Alright, alright. Listen, he let me talk to him about the Lakers for like twenty minutes. He's good by me."

I shake my head. "He would." I look at Garrett and set down the knife. "OK, you want to slice the rest of these pizzas while I start bringing them out?"

When it's time for cupcakes, Agnes sits in my lap, a gigantic pink butterfly painted on one of her cheeks.

About twenty kids—most with basketballs, unicorns, and Blueys now painted on their faces—sit impatiently in front of their decorated cupcakes, most of them half eaten already. Jack emerges from the house holding a rainbow-shaped mini cake I made for Agnes, five candles stuck on top, and passes it to Garrett, who holds it in front of Agnes.

At the conclusion of a rousing rendition of "Happy Birthday," I tell Agnes, "Make a wish!" my voice shaky with emotion, as Garrett tilts the candles toward her. She inhales and blows *hard*. Jack stands a few feet back, beaming, and Stuart bellows, "Brava!"

It's Agnes's birthday, but it might as well be my own. The guilt and worry of feeling like I'm not doing enough or that I'm doing it wrong will never go away. But in this moment, looking at these faces is enough to quiet my mind for now. Agnes probably won't remember this day in ten years, but I will.

The sugar highs come fast, and the come-downs even faster. At the first sign of a tantrum, guests start to pack up. I feel exhausted but accomplished, like I do after my team and I execute a particularly intricate set or a long day of filming.

"Thank you for having us," Tom's wife, Molly, tells me, their daughter conked out in her arms. "Yes, this was inspired," Tom adds at her side. "So well-executed Sabrina is bound to demand one just like it." I laugh as I take in what's left of it: Jack putting cupcake wrappers into a garbage bag, Garrett breaking down pizza boxes, Agnes running around animatedly with her few lingering friends.

"It's not the right moment, I know," I say as I lean in to hug Molly. "But Jack said you're working on a new novel—I want to hear about it next time."

"You say that now," she jokes. "You two will have to come over for dinner soon."

"What about you, CJ? Any upcoming projects?" Tom asks.

"I've been doing some smaller shoots for commercials,

branded work, that sort of thing. Feels more manageable than going straight into another movie."

"Hear, hear," he says.

"I'll probably look for something more substantial in the New Year."

"And what about Jack?" Tom asks.

"*Tom*," Molly *tsk*s.

"What about him?" *Is he asking about my* intentions?

"Well, you managed to do the one thing the rest of us couldn't: convince him there is more to life than work."

I adjust my hair, flummoxed, trying to come up with what to say when I'm rescued by Jack appearing at my side, doling out hugs and goodbyes.

When everyone but Stuart is finally gone, Jack and I pull my green metal patio furniture back into its rightful place in front of the desert willow tree and slump into the chairs. Jack interlaces his hands in his lap, and his thumbs dart one over the other, like he's playing a game of thumb war against himself. He bites the inside of his cheek, and I can tell he's on the precipice of saying something of consequence.

"So." He pulls my leg across his knees. "What's the full story with Garrett?"

I let out a heavy sigh. "We broke up twice—I told you that, right?"

He nods.

"The first time was right when my mom first got sick. You know, I was running around, trying to figure out her health insurance, picking up her medications, taking her to appointments. When he finally asked if there was anything he could do to help, I gave him a grocery list—like an actual grocery list, eggs and stuff. He spent the entire time at the store calling and texting me, just absolutely lost." I move my other leg to Jack's knees as well. "I think, looking back, that he was probably so desperate not to do it wrong because he knew how that would go over, but at the time, I didn't have the capacity to see that, and I only half accept it now."

He bobs his head, playing at a hole in the knee of my jeans.

"And after I started passing up film work so I could bartend, I'd text him updates about what was going on, and I wouldn't hear back for hours. It just felt like, what was the point of having a partner if they weren't there to support me? So, when we got back together after she died, it was really in a moment of grief. It was over by the time I found out I was pregnant with Agnes. I told him that he could be involved—that I was happy for him to be—but I wasn't going to expect anything from him. He said he wanted to help financially and see her on nights and weekends when he wasn't filming. We have a very friendly custody agreement. I trust him, and I know he loves her. But I think he loves to move around too much to settle down and do it for real." Letting this all out, I feel the release of pressure I didn't know I was still holding. Like my ears finally popping after a long flight.

"I'm sorry you went through all of that feeling alone."

He reaches toward me and encircles one of my hands with his own.

"Yeah, well, I learned a lot about how people show up," I say, perhaps more sardonic than I feel.

He looks me square, a serious expression on his face.

"Hey. I promise to show up. But also—you were both young. Maybe Garrett didn't know how to show up then, in a way he seems to now? You know, in an Agnes's dad way."

I crawl into Jack's lap. "Maybe." I sigh, relenting. "You might be right." Little by little, Jack is sanding down the edges of my petulance. I've tried to be less hard on Garrett over the years, but today is the easiest I've been on him, by far. My arms move around Jack's neck; his hands go to my waist.

"Hey, I was thinking if you don't feel like going back to London for the holidays . . . I was wondering if you'd stay here. And spend them with us."

Jack's smile is wide, and we both know it's an acknowledgment of his excitement but also of what it means for me to ask. "We can do Christmas crackers."

At the confused expression on my face, he shakes his head and pulls me closer. "Getting ahead of myself. Yes, I would like that a lot."

I curl into him and tug the sleeve of his chambray shirt.

"Mommy?" I hear from the back door, and Jack and I immediately spring apart.

"Jack can borrow Kristy if he wants," she says, holding

out her favorite stuffed animal, a well-loved giraffe. "To help him sleep." Last night, I'd told Agnes Jack would be staying over after the party. She hadn't reacted, just went on arranging her stuffies on her bed. Now I see that she was processing this milestone not for herself but for him.

Jack recognizes the gesture for what it is. "Agnes, Kristy—it would be my great honor."

XXIII

Jack

"OK, now signal," Tom says as we approach the on-ramp of the 101. "Accelerate—not that much!" He braces his hand against his door as I ease my foot off the gas.

"Sorry, sorry." I check my mirrors and claim my place in the right lane. "Tom, look! I'm merging!"

"And what a job you're doing of it. Have you told CJ yet that you passed your permit test?"

"Tonight," I say, keeping my eyes on the road. "I'm going to show her my driver's permit during Saturnalia."

"Is that what you kids are calling it now?"

"Very funny," I respond, but all I can think is *I'm doing it! I'm driving down a highway! In a foreign country!*

"It's an ancient pagan ritual," I explain. "Stuart's thing."

"You're not doing yourself any favors here," Tom volleys back.

A glance in my rearview mirror tells me that there's a Jeep eager to pass and willing to weave dangerously in order to do so.

I lean my hand on the horn, letting my frustrations be known.

"OK, easy." Tom laughs. "Was that your first honk? Your first road rage?"

"You know what, *it was*."

"Great job. Never would've known it was your first time. Though, it's rather unusual to honk at a car behind you. No matter. Good on you. You've been racking up a lot of firsts lately."

"And what's that mean?" My hands are glued to ten and two.

"Your first, uh, *adult* relationship. First time dating a woman who has a kid."

"Are you going somewhere with this?" I ask. "You don't have to warm me up."

"I just . . . want to make sure you know what you're doing. With Agnes. The stakes are different when there's a kid." He fiddles with the air vent. "I just, uh, want to make sure you're not . . . playing house. That this isn't some phase before you jump back onto the Ascendant Actor World Tour."

"I know what the stakes are. You know how I feel about CJ. And this is the first time I feel like I've been in charge of my life since *Flames*." *It's more than that*, I think. "It's also the first time that I've . . . really felt . . . part of a family."

My eyes swipe quickly toward Tom, who is well aware of my distant relationship with my own parents and brother. I see his expression soften in my periphery.

"They're lucky to have you, Jack."

"Sappy."

"Right, right. Two more exits. We're saving I-5 for another day."

When CJ said "the holidays," I didn't know we would be celebrating three: Christmas for me, Chanukah for CJ, and Saturnalia for Stuart, who, like the ancients before him, has embraced the Roman holiday that celebrates its namesake, the god Saturn. According to Stuart, he is a direct descendant of the emperor Nero, which would also make CJ and Agnes direct descendants of the emperor Nero, but I don't mention this.

"Io, Saturnalia!" Stuart says, pulling me in for a hug and clapping me on the back when I walk through the door on December 17.

"Io, Saturnalia!" Agnes chimes in, jumping up and down.

The pair of them are wearing fir-and-ivy garlands on their heads, clearly constructed by CJ. I picture her researching which plants are traditional and why. Tea lights flicker on the surfaces that are high enough to be out of Agnes's reach. A series of sun-and-star drawings that appear to have been a group effort hang around the doorframe.

CJ appears from the kitchen, drying her hands on her fisherman sweater. I can smell lemons and thyme, and the wholesome coziness—set forth for a holiday I hadn't heard of two weeks ago—threatens to overwhelm me.

She stands on her tiptoes to give me a peck on my cheek. "See anything good today?"

Brent Chase is returning to Los Angeles in the New Year, and for some reason, he wants his home back, giving me a new hobby of house hunting. "Eh, same as usual."

The open houses I visited were unremarkable, places without personality that the agent assured me could be transformed into anything with the right architect-and-designer duo.

After dinner of roast chicken, a date-olive-orange salad, and honeyed wine that Stuart concocted for the occasion, we exchange gifts, sitting cross-legged around the trimmed Christmas tree, the menorah we lit last week on the mantel, the tin foil and dried wax still underneath it. Saturnalia presents are supposed to be intentionally small, tokens of our appreciation for each other.

CJ got Stuart a celluloid print of a Kenneth Anger movie; Stuart got Agnes a velvet bow for her hair; I got Agnes a tiny stuffed Jiji from *Kiki's Delivery Service*; Agnes got us all drawings, originals signed by the artist.

Seated next to me, CJ hands me a small box and watches with anticipation as I rip off the silver paper.

It's a framed needlepoint of a bag of Walkers crisps. Cheese and onion. My favorite. My missing-home comfort food.

"You made this?" I look up at her and feel a tingle in my throat.

She meets my gaze, and I can see how happy it makes her to have moved me in this way. "I did. I thought you could put it in your bedroom at Brent's—or wherever you are—to make it feel a little more like it's yours."

"CJ," I say, and she looks between Agnes and Stuart, waving off any emotional overtures.

I pass an envelope to her. She cocks her head. "A gift certificate?"

"Cash," I joke back. "Oh, go on, just open it."

She pulls out the official document and skims it.

"Did you get your driver's license?" she asks, her eyes wide, her mouth open.

"Well, not just yet, *but* I got my driver's *permit*. I just need to take my road test to get my license."

"How—? When—?"

"With my cable bill as proof of address and Tom as my teacher."

CJ throws her arms around me and kisses me on the mouth.

"*Mommy!*" Agnes shrieks, clapping excitedly at the overt display of romance. Deprived of Disney princesses, this is her fix.

"I can't believe it," CJ says as she pulls away slowly.

"What? That I can very nearly drive?"

"No." She shakes her head. "That you outdid me."

XXIV

Jack

I'm not proud, but it is what it is: I've become addicted to this ludicrously priced juice place in Los Feliz. It's December 22, and the city is emptying out in accordance with the holiday season. All real work put off for a more civilized time: next year.

Which makes it all the more surprising when I see that I have a missed call from Delia while I'm waiting in a shorter-than-usual line for my pressed vegetables. The six months I pledged to take off from work are coming to a close; I have every intention of regrouping with her in January and plotting what's next. To discover how much damage I've done to my career, exactly, and if there are projects filming in LA that might be right for me as a start. I have inside me exactly what was missing six months ago: an ache and hunger to work, a kind I haven't felt since my *Flames* days.

Delia's name on my lock screen makes my stomach sink. *No one* is reaching out on the Friday before Christmas unless it's bad news.

I step out of line and pace outside as I dial her back. I

mentally prepare for her to tell me that, despite the reas-
surances she'd made when we last spoke, she can't keep me
on her roster anymore.

"Jack." Her voice sounds far away.

"Delia, hi!" My voice is strained.

Two women toting yoga mats shoot haughty looks in
my direction for blocking the entrance. When I grimace
in apology, one whisper-asks her friend, "Was that Jack
Felgate?"

"What are you doing right now? Could we meet somewhere?" Delia asks.

My fears are all but confirmed. It makes sense that she
wants to let me go in person. It's only appropriate, after
all these years, I suppose.

"I'm just leaving a juice place—"

"Great. Can you meet me at Dialog Café in about
twenty?"

"I think so, yeah . . ."

"I'll see you then," Delia says and hangs up.

I call a car and try to collect myself. I've never moved
through this world without Delia. In the nine years I've
been working with her, she's had a hand in every decision
I've made professionally and some I've made personally too.
During these months away from the industry, I've wielded
more control over my life, and I think I'm better off for
it, but that doesn't mean I'm ready to lose her guidance
completely. It dawns on me that she's become something
of a mother figure—a realization that's surely deserving of
some further unpacking in a therapy setting.

You'll make a case for yourself, I think as I climb into my Uber.

By the time I meet Delia at her table, I've readied my argument: I'm adaptable. I play well with others. I can bring nuance to unnuanced writing. I've been told I'm charming and that people like the looks of me.

"Jack, I want you to know something," she starts before I've settled into my chair. "I took what you said about taking time away seriously."

"I appreciate that." I am desperate for her to say her piece so I can say mine.

"And that's why I haven't come to you with any parts in any movies or any roles you were offered, even though some of them were *good*." She looks away from me as she says that last part, as if it physically pains her to recount.

"But the very first time we met, do you remember who you told me your dream director was?"

"Cecily Close," I reply, not sure where this is going.

Delia nods grimly. "Cecily Close, the long-retired, shut-in director who we all thought would never make a movie again."

"The very one."

"Well, she's making another movie."

I feel a strange sensation, a tingle up my spine at the thrill of knowing that someday soon, there will be another Cecily Close film. A new work for me to marvel at and watch over and over again.

"That's fantastic. Do you know what it's about?"

"The British rocker Richard Thomson, who was in the band the Birth. They were really big in the '70s and '80s."

"I know that band. They were like a glam rock Sex Pistols. Richard was best friends with Bowie."

A classmate's dad had been one of his roadies and turned us onto the music when I was growing up. We'd put it on after school and shred on air guitars, channeling the energy of rockers readying to stomp around London and chase after girls.

"I'll be there opening weekend."

"No, Jack." Delia looks at me as if I haven't a clue in the world. She searches the faces of the people at the other tables and leans forward conspiratorially. "She wants *you* to be in it."

I open my mouth, but that's as far as I get.

Delia pulls a bound script out of the giant leather bag on the chair next to her and drops it down on the table between us.

"I've read it, Jack, and it's *really* good."

I don't need to read it to know. "I'm in. I'll play whatever, whoever she wants."

I'm going to be in a Cecily Close movie. I'm going to be in a fucking Cecily Close *movie. I can't wait to tell CJ. CJ isn't going to believe this.*

"Jack, she wants you to play the lead."

"Richard fucking Thomson? Are you serious?"

"Jack, yes, I'm serious. And since your six months are just about up, the timing is pretty much perfect."

"Absolutely, I'm in." I am already envisioning meeting with Cecily, getting into character, immersing myself in Richard, and doing his story justice. "Why do you think she thought to cast me? Did they tell you?"

"She saw your work in *Gatsby*. She's close friends with the *original* Gray, Timmy's father. He showed her a cut, and she was impressed."

In that moment, my whole body feels lit up from within. This is exactly what I'd hoped the part in *Gatsby* would set me up for.

"Incredible. When does it start? How long is the shoot?"

"You have to be in London by January 2, and it'll probably be three months, give or take. They're still figuring it out. All of it is happening quickly because it was so difficult to secure the funding, and the production company wants to move as fast as possible."

My shoulders slump. I don't want to spend months away from CJ. Or Agnes. Or Stuart, if I'm being honest. I think about the late nights on set, the time difference, how all-consuming it is to give myself completely to a character. Phone calls and FaceTimes aren't going to cut it. *What would CJ do?* I ask myself.

"Have they chosen anyone for production design yet?"

Delia furrows her brow, then scrolls through her phone, cross-referencing her emails. "I think they're between a few different people, but no final decision yet."

My mind races. "Tell them . . . I'll only do the movie if they hire CJ Ericson as production designer."

"The production designer from *Gatsby*? I can certainly

throw her name into the ring. She's probably already in consideration."

"Great." I nod, trying to keep my cool. *I am going to act in my dream movie with my dream director and my dream production designer, and CJ and I won't have to be apart. We can find temporary childcare for Agnes in London—daycare or a nanny. Maybe Stuart will want to come.*

Delia's voice interrupts my thoughts. "Can I ask why? Why her?"

"She's extraordinary at what she does. Her attention to detail is like nothing I've experienced on any other set, and she keeps everyone honest." Unable to contain myself, I add, "She's also my girlfriend. And I don't want to do it without her."

Delia narrows her eyes, as if with this new information, she sees me in a new light entirely.

"I'll take this back to the producers. Obviously your endorsement will help. I'll be back in touch by end of day. We'll discuss the rest then."

"I'm serious, Delia. You know I'm desperate to do this movie. And I know you think I'd be absolutely mad to turn it down for any reason. But this is my deal-breaker."

Delia narrows her eyes again, like she's adjusting the focus of her lens on me.

It doesn't take until end of day for Delia to confirm: Two hours later, my phone buzzes. "Cecily said yes to both of you," her text reads. Agnes is with Garrett, and CJ and I are sitting on her couch watching *The Shop Around the Corner* when the good news reaches me.

I bite my cheek and grin at CJ.

"What's going on with you? You've had this weird, mischievous look all day."

I grab the remote from her and pause the movie. "You're not going to believe this. I heard from Delia today. Cecily Close is making a movie about Richard Thomson. The British rock star."

"Cecily Close is coming out of retirement? That's unbelievable."

"They offered me the part of Richard Thomson."

CJ's eyes widen.

"Jack! This is huge!" She grabs me by both cheeks and kisses me. "When does it start? Where is it shooting?"

"It starts in a couple of weeks—quick, I know—and we're filming in London—"

Confusion seeps in, muddling the joyful expression on her face. CJ cuts me off before I can finish explaining. "Why didn't you tell me earlier?"

"Because I just found out, and I was waiting for confirmation before saying anything—but they want you on production design."

CJ's face contorts. She pulls away from me, and I am at an absolute loss.

XXV

CJ

"What do you mean, *you were waiting for confirmation*? Why is this information coming through you and not my agent?"

"They offered me the role, and I said I would only do it if you were the production designer."

My heart races. "Jack, how do you know I even *want* the job?"

"I guess I—it's working with Cecily Close! And with me! I thought it was obvious."

I stand up from the couch and walk into the kitchen, the pounding of my heartbeat reaching my ears. *Does he not think I am capable of getting my own jobs?* I remind myself how much he respects my work and what I do. He *likes* that I'm good at what I do.

Jack follows me into the kitchen, and I turn to face him. I know I need to try to hear him out.

"We had so much fun working together on *Gatsby*. And I know there is no one who will do a better job of bringing this story to life than *you*." He grabs my hands and stares at me pleadingly, his eyes unblinking.

I pull my hands out of his, breaking away. I need to be alone with this. I don't want his touch to distort the anger that's building inside me. "Jack, if it shoots in a few weeks, that's barely any prep time. I don't have any idea what Cecily has in mind for the film." I sigh. "And all of that is beside the point. I can't just up and go to London for months. What about Agnes?"

"She can come too," Jack says with so much hope in his voice.

"I can't uproot her like that. No way."

"Stuart could come! He could help."

"Stuart could not come," I counter immediately. "He has a life too! Just like I do." We stand facing each other in the same little room, but it feels like we exist in different realities.

I mull over the details of what he's proposing. Me getting an offer on a giant movie . . . without any kind of conversation with the director or producers beforehand. Without the involvement of my reps.

"Jack," I say crisply. "Did you tell Delia we're dating?"

"Uhh," he stumbles. Wrong answer.

I throw my hands in the air. "How on earth do you think I can walk onto that set and be respected if everyone thinks I'm there because I'm dating the star of the movie?"

"Because you're incredible at what you do, and I'm not the only one who knows it!"

"I wish that was enough, but it's not. Why do you think I wanted to keep it a secret on *Gatsby*? For fun?"

"That was different," he says quietly. "We weren't together yet, and a hookup—I understand that. But now, why does everything have to be a secret? Why are there so many rules?"

"Because things work differently for single-mom production designers than they do for sought-after male movie stars."

"I don't know the point of being a movie star if I can't surround myself with the people I want to work with. This whole business runs on favors. I don't see why this should be any different." He grabs at his hair, and I can feel his frustration coming off of him in waves. I hope he can feel mine.

"Because *I* need to know anything that comes to me is because of my talent. How am I supposed to believe in it otherwise?" I exhale sharply. "Why didn't you ask me or talk to me about it?"

"I got excited and caught up in the moment." He leans back against the counter and props his arms up as if to brace himself. "And probably because I knew you'd never let me put in a good word for you."

"Well, you were right about that." I cross my arms over my chest. There are only a few feet separating us, but it may as well be miles.

"I'm sorry," Jack says. "I won't do the movie. I'll stay here. There will be other offers."

"No." My tone is firm. "You have to take the movie. You absolutely cannot pass this up for me. I will not let you." My anger is subsiding, and sadness is replacing it. I mean what I say to him, but I also can't believe this is happening now, and like this. I thought we'd have time to strategize. That we'd sit down in January and make a plan. I hadn't let myself imagine what it would be like for Jack to reenter his real life so abruptly or how far it would take him from mine.

He dips his head slightly, and he reaches for my wrist.

"Has it ever occurred to you," he asks me slowly, "that I might want to be with you more than I want this role? That you may not know what is best for everyone?"

I swallow hard. My brain feels like it's pushing against my forehead. "That's a funny thing to say, considering you spent today acting like a career counselor on my behalf."

He lets out a sad laugh. "Believe it or not, I thought I was taking a page out of *your* book. I was asking for what I want."

"Without considering how it would affect me." I make a fist and feel the muscles of my arm tighten under his grip. He lets go. I feel both better and worse. "Is that how you think of me? As stubborn and selfish?"

"No!" Jack says, concern washing over his face. "But you know how to stand your ground and make things happen."

"So, the answer to that is yes." My words are bitter now, my anger cresting again.

"I told them I wouldn't do the movie without you." His voice is barely audible.

"You should've thought it through before making a promise you can't keep. Go do the movie," I insist, stepping back into the living room and folding the blanket on the couch. "We can talk when you get back."

"So that's it? One mistake and we'll talk again in three months?" Jack's jaw is set, but his eyes are glassy.

Seeing him on the edge of tears makes me need to fight back my own, but I just shrug, unsure what to say.

"CJ, I know how you're reading this, and I can even see where I went wrong. But you know as well as I do why I did it. Because I love you. And I think you love me too, even if you don't want to say it." With that, Jack strides out of the kitchen, through the living room, and out the door.

XXVI

Jack

Seat belts are fastened, baggage is stowed, tray tables are in their upright and locked position, and the plane is ascending into the California sky, hurtling me toward London. I sigh and look out the window, feeling—for the first time on a flight to Heathrow—that I am leaving home instead of returning to it.

An unspeakable number of hours later, I open the door to a flat that Delia's assistant secured for me for filming. I can't believe I am back here: in another blandly nice short-term rental that leaves me once again rudderless. I used to tell myself that I *liked* this sort of freedom—or perhaps I really did. Having no ties to anywhere, able to pick and leave for a job at a moment's notice, seemed ideal until I learned what it feels like to have someone you don't want to leave behind.

It's Christmas Eve, and all I want to do is wallow. I told Tom I'd be with my family for the holiday, and I told my family that I'd be with Tom in the States. It's a ruse that's left me to my own devices: Strongbow, takeaway, Hitchcock's filmography, tears.

From here, I am off to the races, making a very, very busy schedule out of feeling sorry for myself: waking up around noon, parking myself on the couch, and flipping on the TV. Promising myself just one more movie, just one more, one more movie, as the day slips into night and the next one does too.

When I drag myself into bed, I replay another movie in my head, this one called *Jack Was in a Happy Relationship with a Woman He Loved, and He Fucked It Up*. I see all the things that were right and exactly where I went wrong. I know CJ well enough to know she would hate me involving myself in her work in this way, and I did it anyway, unthinking.

On day three, I charge my phone for the first time since my pity party began. There are texts from my parents asking me how my holiday with Tom was; from Tom asking me how my holiday with my parents was. Messages from friends congratulating me on the casting news. An invite to a New Year's party from Ginny—"want you to meet my new boyf, if that's not awkward." Nothing from CJ.

I ready myself for Delia's barrage. From the 26th: "Hope the prep is going well. Will miss you at *Gatsby* premiere next week. Studio loving the early response. Will be in London next month. Drink then?"

From the 27th: "With all the buzz around *Gatsby* and Cecily Close picture, couldn't hurt to get your name back out there. Let's discuss your event schedule?"

By the 28th, today, she's given up on subtlety and has forwarded media requests and details on parties in London where I can and should be spotted. Jack Felgate, a Man About Town once again.

I roll my eyes and return to the task at hand: choosing my next movie. After days of the same recommendations from the streaming service's highly sophisticated algorithm, it serves me something new: *The Bee's Knees*. CJ's breakout that she refused to watch with me while we were together.

I press play before I can consider how much sadder this might make me, and within minutes, I'm too caught up to worry. It's a live-action movie that incorporates stop-motion elements, like an early Tim Burton, about a young girl who retreats into an imaginary world within her mind. It is rich and inviting, with a color palette like a children's book.

I want to ask CJ how she figured out the right scale for the furniture. I want to quiz her about working with the costume department. I want to thank her for somehow lifting my spirits and making me hopeful about anything at all from five thousand miles away after she unceremoniously showed me the door and cracked my heart clean in half.

I think back on how I searched for her name—Cara—at the end of every film for years after we first met. And how now I know not just her work—and the name she actually goes by—but also everything she worked through to achieve it: mourning her mom, raising Agnes on her own. I think about how someday she might watch this Richard Thomson movie, or probably Stuart will, or, ten years from now, maybe Agnes will. As *The Bee's Knees'* credits roll, a giant pit in my stomach forms: *What the fuck am I doing?* Whether or not CJ wants to be *with* me, I desperately need her to be proud of me. I need to be proud of myself. I need to get it together for this role.

I turn the TV off and flip open my laptop, queuing up articles about Richard Thomson that a PA has been emailing to me since I signed on for the film. I have a week and a half and three Zoom sessions with Cecily to nail down the character before shooting begins. I can do this. For myself, for CJ, for Cecily Close, and for the distant fantasy that if I can prove myself in this job, I never need to let Delia roll me out for a photo op ever again.

XXVII

CJ

"Cut!" the director, Carrie Carpenter, calls out.

"Hey, let me know what you think of this setup." Carrie turns to me, and I tug my seat next to hers behind the monitor to take a look. We're working together on a film about a former mob wife who becomes the mob boss, and tonight's set is a historic old steakhouse downtown that was once a favorite of actual crime families. It was a big coup to secure it, and the locations manager and I worked together to pull it off.

I look up and see that a nearby grip is observing me curiously. I make eye contact, then break it swiftly.

My thoughts drift to Jack, on another set somewhere, halfway around the world. As far as I know.

I silently reprimand myself for letting him take up my attention, but I know by now that never prevents my thoughts from circling back to him only moments later. I haven't had time to grieve this relationship, and I won't. I have work to do. I have Agnes to raise. Being upset about him around her isn't an option. I have enough regret about letting him into her life to begin with.

With that thought, my frustration with him transmogrifies into something else: anger at myself. It's *my fault* for letting him into my life. My fault for dating someone who could impact my career. My fault for falling in love with someone who lives a completely different life and for thinking that maybe it will all just figure itself out when I know better: *I* have to figure things out.

The day after Jack left, knowing how difficult it would be to tell Agnes that he was gone and wanting to rip the Band-Aid off, I woke up early. I did yoga to center myself. I showered. I made pancakes and fried bacon.

"Where is Jackie?" Agnes had asked innocuously as she picked up a square of her chocolate chip pancake and dunked it into the large pool of syrup on her plate.

"Agnes, fork," I instructed as I sat down next to her, preparing. "Jackie isn't going to come over anymore." I smoothed my fingers through her hair to comfort her and felt my throat tighten remembering the tense conversation that took place only a few feet away.

"I'm gonna miss him," Agnes said simply and reached for her utensil.

I rubbed her cheek with my thumb. "I know he'll miss you too."

I felt relief that I got it over with, conveniently forgetting that with a five-year-old, I would be having the conversation again and again.

"Where's Jackie?" she asked from the back seat when I was driving us to the Tar Pits.

"Is Jackie coming?" she asked when we were on our way to see *Aristocats* at the New Beverly.

"Do you still kiss Jackie?" she asked when we were snuggled up in bed.

Each time, it was difficult to tell her the same thing—without detail, both because I didn't know what to say and because I didn't know the point—but it was worse when she stopped asking.

Yet somehow, the conversation with Stuart had been much, much harder.

He came over for Movie Club a few nights after Jack left, and he found me in ratty sweatpants, with unwashed hair and a bad attitude while Agnes played in her room.

"What's going on?" Stuart asked. "Where's Jack?"

"He's gone."

"What do you mean, 'he's gone'?" Stuart sat down next to me on the couch and folded his hands in his lap. "What happened? Why didn't you tell me sooner?"

"He got cast in a Cecily Close film."

"Cecily Close is directing again?" Stuart asked, surprised. "I never thought I'd see the day."

"Neither did I. Neither did he. They offered him the lead, so he's off to London."

"Well, that's fantastic. We should all go out there over Agnes's spring break. I assume you want to visit sooner, though? I'm happy to take care of her here for a week, or she could even stay at mine, if you think she's old enough. The guest bedroom just—"

"We broke up," I pronounced.

"Why?"

"He tried to throw his weight around to get me a job on the movie."

I watched the confusion register on Stuart's face. "So, you broke up because he tried to help you out with a job?"

I nodded slowly.

"Wow, what a monster," Stuart said sardonically.

"It's more complicated than that," I insisted. "Everyone on set would've known that the star was my boyfriend."

"Everyone is someone's boyfriend. Or wife. Or son. For God's sake, look at Timmy Gray—you didn't write him off. I'm not saying you were wrong to turn it down, but at least realize he was only doing what he thought was right. And you have a tendency to . . . push people away."

"I don't push people away," I insisted. "I have high standards, but I don't *push* people away."

"Cara. Darling."

The accusation stung coming from Stuart, who had dipped in and out of my life for three decades before becoming a permanent fixture. "I don't! You're here, aren't you?"

"That's because I forced myself in."

"It's not like you were around when I was growing up for me to have welcomed you then."

Stuart hung his head. "And you know I regret that every day. I *should've* been there. I should've fought harder for you. It was complicated, between your mother and me, but she would want—"

The wound of Jack leaving was much too fresh to put salt in it. "Don't talk to me about what *she* would want."

He saw the hurt in my eyes and retreated. "You're right. I'm sorry. But I have to say, Jack is special. He is not someone you could have planned for, and that it is hard doesn't mean it is not worth it. Take it from someone who took the easy path for far too many years. You're not committing a grave sin by letting this man be part of your life and maybe even change the shape of it."

I don't want to hear Stuart, so I don't. "If you need to get back to your place tonight, don't worry about it," I said, but what he and I both knew I meant was that it was probably a good idea for him to go. He promptly took his leave. *If I push people away*, I thought, *maybe it's because they deserve it.*

After we wrap the scene—early, even—Carrie pulls me aside.

"I appreciated having your input on that. Thank you." Carrie, close to my age with a cropped pixie haircut and big laugh, feels more like a peer than any director I've ever worked with.

"Always happy to. Thank *you* for making this set . . . almost zen."

"It's amazing how that feels like a miracle, when it doesn't have to be." She looks me over, finger to her lip. "OK, I've been wanting to ask: Have you ever thought about directing?"

Since my conversation about it with Jack, the idea has gone from a piece of sand rattling around in my thoughts to a pearl: something smoother and maybe a little precious. But it's been only mine. *What if this is something I actually want? And what if it doesn't work out?*

"I've . . . had the thought." My heartbeat picks up. "I don't know that I'm qualified or where I would start—assistant director, I guess? Production design is always what I saw for myself. But over the years, I've realized that I, uh, certainly have opinions on how other things should be done."

"Well, you should consider it," she says good-naturedly. "It seems like it comes naturally to you. Besides, how many male directors do you know that think they need to keep their heads down and pay their dues?"

We both laugh.

"You know, with *Gatsby* about to be in theaters, I think you're going to have a lot more doors opening for you." I've been surprised, but gratified, at all the positive buzz that Timmy's movie is getting. The studio is doing a limited rollout in select cities as a last-ditch attempt to qualify it for the Oscars; it seems like it could end up being big for all of us, cast and crew.

Through the start-and-stop traffic on my drive home, I think more about Carrie's comment. Maybe it is time for me to make significant considerations about my career. My head swims with the possibilities of what it might be like to helm a movie, to take what I know about creating something from nothing and apply it to scripts and actors. I'd have more control over my schedule. I might be able to take longer breaks from work. I could run sets where everyone feels safe and heard. I could surround myself with no bad actors, in the literal and figurative sense. But I would also have to delegate more than I do as production designer—rely on others to execute my vision. I would have to let more people in.

I turn my key in the lock to our front door. Stuart is asleep on the couch, stubbornly refusing to let our stalemate affect his time with Agnes. All of my resentment and anger with him over our fight a few days earlier is harder to summon in this moment, with him sprawled out, a copy of *Sight and Sound* open on his chest. I gently pull the magazine off him and adjust a throw pillow under his head before making my way to check on Agnes and tuck myself into bed.

XXVIII

Jack

"Cut!" the director—Cecily Close herself—calls out.

We're two hours into today's shoot at a legendary London rock club, restored through movie magic to its dingy roots, an instance where scores of people and loads of budget were deployed to make something look worse. This scene is the emotional linchpin of the film and kicks off our busiest day of shooting so far, now three weeks in.

I am tucked into a booth surrounded by the actors playing Richard's bandmates, some of whom would go on to become bold names themselves and others who Richard left behind in Hackney. The plan for the day is ambitious: to film Richard and his friends shooting the shit like it's a regular night out, while Richard takes in a concert in the background and becomes so enraptured by the music that he gets up to walk through the crowd and climbs onto the stage. The beginning of his musical ascent. From there, we'll jump forward in time to film the scene wherein Richard actually does realize his dream of playing the Electric Ballroom, quickly changing out costumes for the extras so it's not obvious to viewers that they're seeing the same audience from the previous scenes.

Since filming kicked off, I've felt confident, competent. Able to focus, despite everything—or maybe because refusing to acknowledge my life beyond the set feels like a survival instinct right now. But something is off today. Cecily has called cut an as-yet-unprecedented fifteen times, and we haven't even broken for lunch.

"Back to one, everybody!" the assistant director instructs.

"No, no, no. What would be the point of going back to one if we haven't fixed the problem at hand?" Cecily digs into the pocket of her chore coat and pulls out not a pack but a single loose cigarette. It is thin and limp, and it occurs to me it might be older than I am.

"You can't smoke in here," the assistant director whispers to her.

"I know you can't smoke in here. I'm old, not *dead*. I've been to pubs and restaurants in the last thirty years."

"Then, why . . ."

"I want to *hold* a cigarette. They haven't outlawed that as well, have they? Am I allowed to hold a cigarette while I think?"

The assistant director appears to actually ponder this for a moment. "I guess you are."

Cecily spots a young crew member nearby pulling on his vape as discreetly as possible.

"Can I just say, it's *absurd* that smoking indoors is illegal and *that* is perfectly tolerated."

The crew member attempts to somehow swallow back the mist he's already puffed into the air.

"No, by all means. At least *one* of us should get to enjoy the satisfaction only nicotine can provide." Everyone laughs. "If we get any further behind schedule, I might ask you to stand closer to me and blow some my way."

This is a nothing exchange—there are dozens like it every day. Each one exactly this charming. Which is to say: Cecily Close is everything I always hoped she would be.

"Jack, could I speak with you for a moment?" Cecily points her fag at me.

Fuck.

"The rest of you: Take five," Cecily announces from her seat.

"Should we make it a cool twenty?" the assistant director chimes in. "So that we can count it toward the union mandate?"

Cecily looks almost disturbed by the inanity of the question. She throws her hands up. "Sure, why not?"

Cecily walks past me and says over her shoulder, "Why don't you and I step outside?"

It's a blustery London winter day, a shade of gray I've only ever seen in this city. Waiting by the door for me, Cecily is wiry and birdlike but somehow larger than life. This is a woman who's directed Oscar-winning performances, who helped define the filmmaking sensibilities of the '70s and '80s, who's made James Cameron cry. And she walked away from all of it to have a private life and raise her daughter.

"Dreadful, isn't it?" she asks, gesturing abstractly ahead of us.

"Well, is there such a thing as good London weather?" I respond generically. *I'm nervous.*

"No, I mean, what's happening to this neighborhood. I think I saw a group of women drinking martinis made with coffee—disgusting." She pulls out a matchbook from her pocket, now actually lighting her cigarette and taking a drag.

"I hope I'm allowed to smoke *out here*." She looks around, then sighs. "When you're young, you never expect the world to change so much. This club was like another home to me for so many years."

"Really?" I ask, surprised.

"Oh, yes." Cecily laughs, then pauses, as if caught in the reverie. "I came and took pictures of all the bands, anyone who would let me."

I'd known Cecily had gotten her start as a photographer before she transitioned to filmmaking. But I wouldn't have guessed a club like this one would have been her stomping ground.

"Jack," she starts again. "I want to tell you something. For some time now, I'd been wanting to make this film about Richard, but I needed every single piece to fall into place correctly, and it seemed like it might never happen. I wasn't sure if there would be anyone who could capture Richard's essence so clearly. I saw you in *Mother Courage and Her Children* all those years ago . . ."

Cecily Close saw me in that play?

"I knew you had a lot of promise then, and I've followed your career ever since. When I saw the early *Gatsby* cut, it confirmed what I already knew: that you are *the* actor to play Richard."

I register the way she refers to him only by his first name, a certain familiarity and weight to it—the sort of one-sided intimacy with a character that develops when a director has been poring over a dream project for this long.

"But here we are, and something's missing. I need you to be honest with me: Do you think you can do this?" My stomach lurches as I process what she's saying.

"I know I can," I say. Quickly, decisively. Doing this role justice is, frankly, all I have right now.

"Then, what in the name of God is going on here?"

"Well, what . . . can I ask . . . what do you mean?" After snapping myself out of my holiday doldrums, I'd taken my prep seriously. I watched interviews. I screened the iconic Richard Thomson concert documentary directed by Jonathan Demme. I feverishly ordered a guitar so I could familiarize myself with the weight of it in my hands. I *felt* ready.

"I mean that . . . you're doing a competent job, but it's like you're painting by numbers. There's something missing or something on your mind. You're elsewhere instead of here."

A wave of shame washes over me. Before I can respond, Cecily continues.

"Forgive me if this is presumptuous, but does it have to do with the production designer? The one who you said wanted the job, then as it turns out, didn't want the job? I have to say, that was quite the back-and-forth."

I consider whether it's worth being honest with this director—who I respect more than almost anyone—about my love life. *Fuck it,* I think. *What on earth do I have to lose?*

As I take her through the ups and downs of my and CJ's story, from our initial chance meeting, to our reconnection on the *Gatsby* set, to our subsequent split, Cecily is silent and unreactive. Midway through my story, she stamps out one cigarette and lights another.

I can't help but gush. "She's someone I know I can trust to be honest with me. She's headstrong and bold but somehow still kind . . . I just . . ." I'm rambling.

Cecily's eyes narrow underneath her long gray-silver bangs.

"Jack, have you ever walked onto set and been made to feel like you don't belong there?"

I consider her question. I've been anxious on set, felt pressure to prove myself, but no one has made me feel like I don't belong. "No, I guess not."

"Speaking, you know, as a 'woman in Hollywood'"—she uses her fingers to gesture scare quotes, her cigarette ashes scattering as she does—"and one well over forty at that, let me tell you something: There is always going to be someone in this industry looking to undermine you. If you give them the slightest bit of thread, they'll grab hold of it with their grubby little hands and pull with all their might. I would've been delighted to hire CJ based on her experience, but I can understand why she didn't want the job."

"Right, well, I fucked up."

"Well, did you try to fix it? Did you make a grand gesture? Did you fight for her?"

I think back to our argument in her kitchen. I left for London a few days later without exchanging another word.

"No," I admit sheepishly. "I didn't."

Cecily rolls her eyes, and I fear I've been deemed as despicable as the dreaded espresso martinis.

"Now, Jack Felgate, you listen. You have to understand that she has a different way of doing things than you. And that you're going to bump up against each other, but you can't quit because of"—she waves the hand not holding what is now her third cigarette—"logistics."

She pauses and exhales. "I'm going to tell you something else. And it's something not many people in this world know. Or at least not many living ones."

She reaches into the pocket where she stores her cigarettes and pulls out a 4 × 6 photograph, folded in half, and hands it to me. This is definitely older than I am.

"I suppose your generation probably doesn't even know what these are anymore," Cecily remarks with icy mirth. "It's called a photograph, and they used to be actual, physical things."

I let out a laugh, a real one, for what feels like the first time in ages. The black-and-white portrait of Richard Thomson is the most famous one of him ever taken. He's looking directly into the camera, like he's refusing to blink. His hand is propped underneath his chin, and he's wearing a shirt with the first few buttons undone and a loose-fitting denim jacket over that. This picture is the cover of his self-titled album—his most well-known—and what an entire generation of young men showed their barbers for reference for several years in the '80s. It is also the picture that every website ran above his obituary when he passed away a number of years ago.

"I took that photo," Cecily says.

I consider myself something of a Cecily Close scholar, and still this is news to me.

"I gave Richard permission to use it however he saw fit on the condition that I wasn't credited. We were in love for many years," she says, her voice lower now. "And we kept it a secret from everyone. I didn't want anyone to know that I took that picture, because I didn't want to be known as Richard Thomson's bird—like so many of those other women were, plenty of whom had their own real talent, by the way." She wags a finger at me for emphasis. "I wanted to be Cecily Close. And so we always put our relationship second, and eventually, that tore us apart. We thought when we got older, we'd have all the time in the world. Then, he was gone." She says this plainly, staring down at the pavement underfoot.

"When I found out I was pregnant and left everything behind, I knew exactly what everyone would say once I was out of earshot." She rolls her eyes again. "That I was too temperamental, that they didn't think I could handle the *rigors* of filmmaking. But the truth is, I was behaving that way because I was deeply unfulfilled. I was living for work instead of myself. I had to find my way back to real life before

I could step back on a set, and I suggest you do the same for yourself before it's too late. At the end of the day, your life should be your passion, every part of it, not just what we do here, making silly little films."

Cecily flicks her final cigarette on the ground and stamps it out. She walks to the back door of the club, then turns to me.

"And by the way, half of Richard's songs *are* about me." She cocks her head toward me to join her. "I trust you have what you need now."

XXIX

CJ

It's 5:20 a.m., and Agnes and I are sitting on the floor of her bedroom in our pajamas surrounded by Magna-Tiles when Brianna calls.

"Are you freaking out?" She sounds like she's been awake for hours.

"I'm not freaking out, because I'm not going to be nominated," I say, playing it off. But I'm buzzing. I woke up without an alarm at 4 a.m. in anticipation of the Oscar announcements and tidied for a half hour until the force of my nervous energy woke up Agnes. The producers submitted me for *Gatsby*, and the odds are extremely remote—but the big question of *what if* still lodged itself in my system.

"I don't hear your TV."

"They don't start for ten minutes."

"You're infuriating." That's Brianna's way of saying goodbye.

I look up to see Stuart in the doorway with a tote bag over his shoulder. "What are you doing here?" I ask him, surprised. He's not set to drop off Agnes this morning.

"You think I don't know what day it is?"

I sigh and shake my head. "Come on," I say to Agnes as I make my way to my feet. "Let's find out if Mommy got nominated for an Oscar." I let Stuart answer the inevitable flurry of five-year-old questions that follow and focus instead on breathing and managing my expectations.

I queue up the nomination livestream for the three of us, allowing this morning to be a détente for Stuart and me. It's none other than Ginny Friedrich who appears on-screen to read the nominations alongside an equally attractive male counterpart: her costar in an upcoming gender-swapped *Dirty Dancing* remake. I feel a lump form in my throat as my mind races to the most predictable place: *Has Ginny been in touch with Jack lately? Did he reach out to her for comfort? Are there new photos of them at some posh London restaurant, her hand on his knee?*

My stomach flip-flops as we crawl closer to my category. I am about to have either a career-defining moment or the mild satisfaction of telling Brianna I was right.

"CJ Ericson, *The Great Gatsby*." I hear the words come out of Ginny's mouth, and they sound like a spoof. Like the name must secretly belong to someone else, because it can't be *me*. I never thought I'd be so happy to hear my name come out of my ex's ex's mouth.

"There she is!" Stuart crows, clapping his hand on my back. I pull Agnes in for a hug and give her a big kiss on the cheek.

"Yayyyy!" she yells, not really sure what we're celebrating but visibly happy to see me happy and delighted that we're allowed to be this loud this early in the morning.

Stuart pulls a bottle of Dom Perignon from his bag and presents it to me. "After celebratory waffles for us all, *you* will enjoy this, and *I* will take Agnes to school."

We sing along to show tunes as I mix the batter. Stuart makes a batch of whipped cream because "if not now, when?" and Agnes successfully petitions for hot chocolate too. But after breakfast, when Stuart shepherds Agnes out the door and they are gone, I look around our empty house and a surge of emotion and exhaustion overtakes my body without warning. With a deep, guttural wail, I begin to cry.

An hour later, Stuart is back, and this time, he has cappuccinos. "*Congratulations to you, congratulations to you,*" he sings to the tune of "Happy Birthday." Until he sees me.

I am sunken into the couch, tears still flowing. Every time I think I'm done, another sob gets caught in my chest and fights its way out of me.

"Oh, honey," he says, sinking to my side and wrapping an arm around me to pull my head to his chest.

With his free hand, he grabs the box of tissues next to the couch and offers it to me. I take one and press it to my face, as much to hide it as anything. I am profoundly grateful that Stuart does not ask what's wrong. I am unprepared to answer and even more unprepared to admit he may not have been entirely wrong in our fight.

He sits in silence, waiting patiently. I steady my breath and blow my nose, but I don't say anything.

"Do you think, then, maybe, this is about Jack?" Stuart finally asks. I can tell he's worried about what saying this might do to me and whether I might expel him from my house, like I did last time.

When I open my mouth to speak, my throat is sore and my voice raspy. "When I got the news, all I could think was, *I have to call Jack*. That no one will understand this like he will or be happier for me than he will. And when I realized I couldn't . . ." I trail off. The sight of me now tells the rest of the story.

Stuart interlaces his hands on his lap. "There are some days I look at you and all I can see is your mother."

The tears return fast, but they're quieter this time.

"I say this with all the love and respect in the world for her, but she was an 'all-or-nothing' person, and she didn't want me around if I couldn't be there for you as a father in . . . a traditional sense. You've done such an incredible job building this career for yourself and raising Agnes. And I know how capable you are of doing anything you set your mind to. There is no one I believe in more to do the things they say they're going to do or that I trust to handle something. But just because you *can* do all of this by yourself . . . it doesn't mean you have to. Or that you should. Or that you're better off for it." Stuart pauses, but he isn't done. "I know you've been cross with me, and I understand you like to do things your way and need to come around to things in your own time. But I would hate to see you give up on something that's made you the happiest you've ever been because someone might not be the superhuman that you are."

I roll my eyes, but I feel the corners of my mouth turn up as I reach for another tissue.

"Some of us," Stuart says, his expression sharper now, "are just mere mortals. Even those who also happen to be handsome, debonair movie stars. Jack is a mortal in the very best way, I think. In a way that is good for you."

For years, I've taken Stuart's needling about doing less, letting my hair down more, as unserious—his devil-may-care persona on display. But today it sounds more like the pointed advice of a person who's known me my entire life, a person who has been my rock since my mom died and Agnes was born.

I shift from my seat on the couch and wrap my arms around his torso, leaning my head on his chest and hugging him in. He squeezes me back and gently strokes the top of my head.

My tears have a new feeling now. "Thank you," I say softly. "And thank you for being my dad."

XXX

Jack

On my left is Charlize Theron. On my right, Mahershala Ali.

I've been in plenty of scenarios like this before, but it's my very first time at the Oscars. Nothing else quite compares.

Knowing that she is sitting somewhere in the rows behind me gnaws at my focus. That we are in the same place, at the same time, and not together—my body knows how wrong that is, and I can't quite get comfortable in my seat. I want her next to me, telling me what she *really* thought of all the movies that are up for awards this year. I want her hand in mine, her nails digging into my skin a little as we wait for her category to be called.

I got wind of the nominations during a break in filming and hurried online to send her a bouquet. But then I went to fill out the note, and everything I had to say required more space than there was room on the card. After a full hour in my trailer, I landed on "Well done. No one deserves this more." I didn't want to overstep or to have the conversation over typed missives in any medium. But that didn't stop me from anxiously checking my texts for a message from her for days after. None came. *She probably figures Delia's assistant ordered the flowers anyway.*

As the show starts and the chatter quiets, I wipe my palms on the legs of my navy tux. *This is it,* I promise myself. *No matter what happens tonight, I'm going to find her—and do whatever it takes to get her back.*

Conscious of the cameras panning the first few rows, I focus on the program as best as I can, performing the role of Good-Natured Actor Who Is Excited to Be Here. Between categories, when the show cuts to an ad break and everyone around me mingles, I crane my neck to see if I can spot CJ with the rest of the *Gatsby* crew. No luck.

About an hour in, it's time: Her category is up. I sit tall in my seat as Natasha Lyonne and Sterling K. Brown do some light banter about how they never feel more alive than during *sets*—"sets" being an obvious play on "sex." *Sets* are what make them feel alive. No matter how hard they try, they can never get enough *sets.* The bit is all of thirty seconds, but it feels like it lasts a lifetime. I drum my fingers against my leg and tap the heel of my shoe.

My heart contracts as Natasha reads out "CJ Ericson, *The Great Gatsby*" among the nominees.

"And the Oscar goes to . . ." Sterling K. Brown begins.

The *chhhhh* sound of the opening of the envelope. The tug of the card from its sleeve. The two sets of eyes reading what it says.

My ears perk up, willing to hear CJ's name.

"Daniela Harrelson, *The Burst Nectar*," they recite in unison.

All around me, applause breaks out. I bring my hands together and clap slowly, playing the part of a good sport.

As Daniela makes her way down the aisle to accept her award, I scan again to see if I can finally get eyes on CJ. I want to hold her hand and tell her it's OK to be upset and that if she doesn't want to let herself, I will be on her behalf.

I don't hear anything Daniela says during her speech. I am busy plotting my escape. As soon as the ceremony cuts to yet another commercial, I "pardon me, pardon me" all the way to the aisle, then make my way out of the auditorium and toward the bar, which is growing busier as the night wears on.

I spot her instantly. She's wearing a pale-yellow silk dress. It's nearly the same color as her hair, but the liquid smoothness of it contrasts sharply with her wild waves, worn loose and free. Her eyes are focused, taking in the liquor being poured in front of her. I want to stride up behind her, wrap an arm around her waist, pull her hair to the side, and press my lips into the warm skin just behind her ear.

Instead, I watch from a distance as she and Brianna clink together two shot glasses, knock them back, and wince as they bite into lime wedges. Seeing her do something so ordinary drives me crazy, and I have to acclimate to the sight before I dare approach.

Brianna spots me and flicks CJ on the arm. CJ, who is

using the back of her hand to blot the corner of her mouth, looks over to me and uses her wrist to try to shield her smile.

I have gotten a smile.

Brianna whispers something in CJ's ear, then starts back for the auditorium, nodding her head at me as she does, like she might be rooting for me, even.

As I approach CJ, my palms are slick. *When do I tell her I'm sorry?* "You were robbed," I blurt out, a little too loudly when she's within earshot.

"Some other time," she says, playing it off.

I have to actively work to thwart the instincts that are telling me we should be touching right now, that every part of our bodies should be as close as possible.

Now, I think.

"CJ, I have to apologize—" I start.

She cuts me off by shaking her head. I can feel my face fall.

She unzips her clutch and pulls out a piece of paper, creased crisply into quarters. She hands it to me. *Am I being passed a note?*

"My speech," she says.

My jaw opens, closes.

"Of *course* I wrote a speech." She laughs at herself and nods at me to proceed.

I unfold the paper.

"I'm so honored to be accepting this award. I want to thank the Academy—I've always wanted to say that—the Gatsby art department, the whole cast and crew, our intrepid director Timmy Gray, our producers, and the many, many filmmakers whose work has provided the inspiration that's gotten me where I am today. No one is an island, and certainly not me. I wouldn't be here today without the love and support of four very important people: my daughter, Agnes; my father, Stuart Blitz; my extraordinary late mother, Jean Ericson; and the man who showed me that the beauty of a passion project is that it doesn't have to be flawless to be perfect—even if I wasn't ready to see that at the time. Thank you."

I drop the hand holding the paper to my side and reach for her wrist with the other.

CJ surveys the area, scanning who will see this, and what they'll assume. Most attendees have made their way back to the auditorium now that the telecast has begun again, but there are a few who lost in their categories and are settling in at the bar.

She locks eyes with me briefly and then starts off toward a nearby hallway.

I trail her down several flights and through a set of labyrinthine passageways, my heart racing and every cell in my body on high alert, until we are in some sort of small, dark side room.

She flips on the light to reveal a beige-carpeted room with a lit mirror and vanity.

"What is this?"

"One of the old dressing rooms in the Grauman's, next door to the Dolby."

"How did you know this was here?"

She takes a tentative step toward me. "I miss you, Jack.

So much. And I'm sorry I pushed you away." Her eyes fall to the ground as she says this, then they find mine.

I shake my head. "No, I'm sorry. I got so wrapped up in the excitement of the Cecily movie and the possibility of being able to share it with you, that I didn't consider how wrongheaded my approach was. It was unthinking. And selfish." I sigh. "One of the things I love about your life and my life with you is that it's . . . tethered. It's not—it doesn't just drift wherever a strong breeze takes it. I fucked up, and then I didn't even have the gumption to fight for you, which is maybe the most humiliating part of this whole thing. When I left . . ." I shake my head at myself. "Every gesture from the other side of the ocean felt lame and tepid, including and perhaps especially sending a bouquet of daisies."

"Those were from you? There was no name on the card." Her eyes are soft.

Right. After all of that, I forgot to sign the card. I can't help myself. I bring my thumb to her cheek and my palm to her jaw. She leans into my hand, closes her eyes, and then grabs my lapel and pulls me to her, kissing me deeply. What starts as something slow and romantic quickly shifts to something more furious, more frantic, more revealing of the ways in which we've starved in each other's absence. She pulls us apart to step backward and sit on the edge of the vanity. She leans back against the mirror and I pull her arms over her head, pin them there with my right hand, and kiss her down her elbow, across her shoulder, along the strap of her dress.

"Fuck," CJ exhales. "Jack, can we try this again?"

I slide my hand over her neck and dip two fingers down the front of her dress, just shy of her nipple. "CJ, it's all I want."

"How many categories do we have until you have to present?" she asks, and I grin into her hair. I inhale like it's my first real breath in months.

"Probably about seven. Though I'm certain Elizabeth Olsen could open an envelope without me." I take her nipple with my thumb and forefinger and squeeze, producing a sharp gasp from her open lips.

She lifts her dress up around her waist and tilts her hips so she can frame me with her legs. "Plenty of time."

My erection is threatening to destroy the seam of my pants, and CJ's hand is at my fly, unzipping it and pulling my dick out of my briefs. She smiles down at it, clearly smug at having made me this hard, then dips her head to take it in her mouth for just a moment before wrapping her hand around me with a slow stroke. I push the soaked wisp of fabric serving as her underwear to the side, but as I reach to feel the wetness between her legs, she grabs my hand and stops me. My chest clenches.

She gives me a coy, bossy look. "Take your clothes off and lay them out there," she says, pointing to the makeup chair. "So that when you get onstage, you don't look like you just got fucked in a dressing room."

"Say I want to look like I just got fucked in a dressing room," I reply, but I'm pulling off my jacket and smoothing it over the seat before I finish the statement. It takes me longer than it should to undo all the shirt buttons because neither of us is willing to break eye contact as I do. By the time I reach my cuff links, she is sliding one hand between her legs, tormenting me by picking up where she cut me off moments earlier. I nearly trip as I bend down to deal with my laces, and she smirks in response but doesn't stop.

When, stark naked, I reach to pull off the straps of her dress, she presses her fingertips down my back and pulls my pelvis against hers. "This we can make a mess of," she says. "I picked it out for you."

My whole body goes molten, and I moan at first contact. I slide against her, and my dick finds her opening on its own, like it knows the way. Because it does.

I brace a hand against the wall as I start thrusting, and she wraps a leg around my waist and scrapes her nails down my neck. I hope she leaves marks. *I hope the cameras pick them up.* Her eyes are closed, lids fluttering. Doing this again feels so right. I can't believe we ever stopped, that I let that happen.

I angle my body so I'm pressing against her clit, the way I know she likes it, the way I know she'll come, and every part of her grips me tighter and pulls me closer. "Jack—" she gasps, and her reaction makes me want to crack us both open. My hip presses against her inner thigh, spreading her wider still.

She cries out like she's forgotten where we are, and it's enough to send me over the edge. Panting into her neck, clutching her body against mine, I feel more at home than I have in years—here in this country that's not my own, in this dressing room I didn't know existed an hour ago, in the arms of this person who makes me feel steady, grounded, and seen.

I kiss her across her jaw, her cheek, her forehead as we both steady ourselves and properly take in this room for the first time. The quiet of this space compared to the cacophony of the ceremony we left behind feels loud in its own way. I taste and smell her on me, a sensory experience I've desperately missed. I want to live here, in this perfect moment. But I have to put my suit back on. I have to be a semblance of the Jack Felgate that people think they know. Which feels easier to do now that the person who genuinely sees me is here.

"You know," she says, her mouth pressed to my ear. "We probably just had sex in the very same place as Charlie Chaplin."

I laugh and nuzzle her neck. "Wow, and if I wasn't hot before."

When I put my suit back on, she adjusts my bow tie, and we head back upstairs, where I arrive just in time to present the award for Best Original Song. We don't even stick around for them to announce Best Picture.

XXXI

CJ

No Governor's Ball, no Vanity Fair Party. For us, the after-party is Brent Chase's house.

"Thank God this man has so many fictional cold cases to solve," I say, pulling on my favorite old, worn uni shirt of Jack's and joining him on the couch. His arms are stretched across the back of it, and his bow tie is on the coffee table.

"I love seeing you in that." He pulls my feet onto his lap and begins to massage them. "Almost as good as the fancy dress. And both in one night . . ." He brings my ankle to his lips to kiss it. "I can't believe you had me in your mouth ten minutes before my first Oscars presenting gig."

"I can't believe we just ditched the Oscars," I say, and I realize I haven't had more than a moment to start to process the lows and highs of the evening.

"I would ditch a lot more than that if you wanted me to."

I shake my head. "That's not—" I stop myself and sit up straighter, determined to articulate my feelings clearly and with intention, both for him and for myself. "Look, I know I can be . . . rigid. And I use Agnes as an excuse to make rules for myself—rules that I really did think my life required. Obviously, Agnes does need structure, and I can't just fly us to London or wherever the next enticing job is shooting. But I can do things that take me out of my comfort zone. Take on projects outside of LA, try directing because I think I could like it and be good at it. Agnes has summers and breaks. And I have Stuart, as he has been quick to remind me."

I trace Jack's jaw with my thumb while I talk, and he reaches up to still my hand and moves it to his lips. "I don't want to make your life harder, CJ. I just want to be with you."

"I know that. I want that. I want *you*." The relief of telling him this unlocks something in me, an ease I'd been avoiding. I continue, without considering what I say before I say it, a behavior so rare for me that it feels terrifying, but right. "I think I got so used to things being hard that I started to take comfort in it, and letting in anyone who made things different—and potentially easier—felt wrong somehow. Getting accustomed to you helping me with little stuff, like planning the birthday party or picking up breakfast—it just seemed like such a short leap from that to you helping me with something big, like the Cecily movie. It scared me. It made me worry that I might not be capable of doing any of it again on my own. Breakfast or booking jobs."

I don't realize I'm crying until I feel Jack wipe a tear from my cheek. "You are the most capable person I know," he says. "I would trust you with the nuclear codes. British and American." He pulls my head to his shoulder. "I want to learn how to be here for you in ways that aren't scary."

"I know," I say, nodding against him. "I always depended on my mom, and then when she was gone . . . I think it felt like a betrayal of her memory to count on anyone but myself. Which—I know how it sounds when I say that out loud. I thought all of my rules were protecting me, but when you left, I saw they were actually isolating me, and Agnes too."

My gaze finds the clock for the first time since we got here, and I realize that Agnes will be up in a few hours. "I need to leave soon," I say, slouching into the couch and resting my head on his chest.

He nods. "I'd like to see her soon if you're OK with that." Jack smooths my hair.

"I'd like that. Agnes would really like that. But also, Jack, I want to make a plan," I start and catch myself. *It's not just about me. It's about us.* "Or—can *we* make a plan? Because working together again *was* a good idea. Even if I didn't think you went about it the right way."

He laughs, and I feel it in his chest. "Brilliant idea, miserable execution on my part."

"The thing is, we would have to be equals. Partners. Not a movie star and his girlfriend."

He nods. "Like Christopher Nolan and Emma Thomas."

"Where you're Emma and I'm Christopher." I smile up at him.

"Obviously. And of course you'll be a bigger success than that bloke. What's he done anyway?"

My laughs evolve into a yawn, and Jack pulls my head

into his lap as my body melts into the couch. "I'm getting too comfortable."

"No such thing. Set an alarm, and I'll take you home whenever you need."

"I, too, can order an Uber."

"No, in my *car*."

I attempt, unsuccessfully, to search his face while looking at it upside down.

"It's quite sensible. Family-friendly. In case there's ever a reason for a small child to ride in the back seat. Brent Chase said I can keep it here until I sign the lease on my new place in Highland Park next month."

Warmth spreads through my chest. "You'll drive me," I say dreamily as my eyelids drop.

"I think you'll rather like seeing me behind the wheel."

You've finished this book, but CJ and Jack's story is just beginning. Read where they go from here in the epilogue, score your The Just OK Gatsby sweatshirt, and get a taste of *Flames Flicker Eternal*, even. Scan here or visit 831stories.com/setpiece.

ACKNOWLEDGMENTS

First and foremost, an enormous, never-ending thank you to Erica Cerulo and Claire Mazur for the beautiful, romantic, and expansive world you're building with 831 Stories and for inviting me to be part of it. I am in awe of you both. And thank you to everyone on the 831 Stories team who touched this book in one way or another, transforming it from a draft into a real, physical thing and ensuring that romance readers have the cutest merch around.

Thank you to Jen Prokop for your keen, insightful edits and all of your feedback to help me bring the world of *Set Piece* into clearer focus. And thank you to Sanjana Basker for your sensitivity read and early words of encouragement.

Thank you to my agent, Susan Raihofer, for your guidance, warmth, and wit and to my friend Carrie Wittmer for making the connection.

My fellow writing group members Leigh Cesiro and Elizabeth Teets, thank you for your discerning eyes and bullish senses of humor. You are the reason I now look forward to Monday nights. I have been explicitly forbidden from sharing the name of our group chat here, but know it's a good one.

Thank you to prop master extraordinaire Scott Lamica for gut-checking and fact-checking what it's like to work in the art department of a Major Hollywood Production.

Thank you to Emma De Matteo, my friend and fellow cinephile, for confirming all of my film references were on the mark and for always being my go-to movie buddy.

Thank you to my former roommate Matt Mancini for showing me firsthand the beauty of the Burbank Costco and the San Fernando Valley at large. 638 Lorimer Street forever.

If you are even a little bit interested in learning more about production design or perhaps the secret and/or forgotten history of Hollywood's first century, I cannot recommend enough Karina Longworth's seminal podcast *You Must Remember This*. The very fictional CJ could not exist had there not been the very real Polly Platt, and the season of *YMRT* dedicated to telling her story was instrumental in shaping CJ and this book at large.

To my dad, thank you for being so proud of me that you tell everyone you meet about my work. And for—no matter what—always having a pen and flashlight on hand.

My biggest cheerleader is, and always has been, my sister Stacy. Thank you for reading everything I write and for steadfastly believing in me so that I don't always have to.

Thank you to Nora Nealis, to whom this book is dedicated—the sharpest, smartest cookie there ever was.

Finally, everything I do always has a piece of my mom in it, and that means this book is no exception. My love and gratitude remain unwavering.

ABOUT THE AUTHOR

LANA SCHWARTZ is a writer born and raised in New York City, where she continues to live today. Her writing has appeared in *The New Yorker*, *McSweeney's*, *The Onion*, *Shondaland*, *Slate*, and more. Her first book, *Build Your Own Romantic Comedy: Pick Your Plot, Meet Your Man, and Direct Your Happily Ever After*, was named one of *Vulture*'s Best Comedy Books of the Year in 2020.

ALSO FROM 831 STORIES